A Bean and Cheese Taco Birthday

Un cumpleaños con tacos de frijoles con queso

By / Por

Diane Gonzales Bertrand

Illustrations by / Ilustraciones de

Robert Trujillo

Spanish translation by / Traducción al español de

Gabriela Baeza Ventura

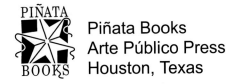

PIÑATA BOOKS

Piñata Books
Arte Público Press
Houston, Texas

Publication of *A Bean and Cheese Taco Birthday* is funded by grants from the City of Houston through the Houston Arts Alliance and the Texas Commission on the Arts. We are grateful for their support.

Esta edición de *Un cumpleaños con tacos de frijoles con queso* ha sido subvencionada por la Ciudad de Houston por medio del Houston Arts Alliance y Texas Commission on the Arts. Les agradecemos su apoyo.

Piñata Books are full of surprises!
¡Piñata Books están llenos de sorpresas!

Piñata Books
An Imprint of Arte Público Press
University of Houston
4902 Gulf Fwy, Bldg 19, Rm 100
Houston, Texas 77204-2004

Cover design by / Diseño de la portada por Bryan Dechter

Bertrand, Diane Gonzales.
    A Bean and Cheese Taco Birthday / by Diane Gonzales Bertrand ; illustrations by Robert Trujillo ; Spanish translation by Gabriela Baeza Ventura = Un cumpleaños con tacos de frijoles con queso / por Diane Gonzales Bertrand ; Ilustraciones de Robert Trujillo ; traducción al español de Gabriela Baeza Ventura.
    p   cm
    ISBN 978-1-55885-812-1 (alk. paper)
    [1. Birthdays—Fiction. 2. Parties—Fiction. 3. Brothers—Fiction. 4. Hispanic Americans—Fiction. 5. Spanish language materials—Bilingual.] I. Trujillo, Robert, 1979- illustrator. II. Ventura, Gabriela Baeza, translator. III. Title. IV. Title: Cumpleaños con tacos de frijoles con queso.
PZ73.B4427 2015
[E]—dc23
                                                                                    2015000891
                                                                                    CIP

Printed in Hong Kong in May 2015–July 2015
by Book Art Inc. / Paramount Printing Company Limited
12 11 10 9 8 7 6 5 4 3 2 1

To my nephews Niall and Connery MacRae with love.
—DGB

To my son, who inspires me to tell great stories and to make yummy burritos.
—RT

Para mis sobrinos Niall y Connery MacRae con cariño.
—DGB

Para mi hijo, quien me inspira a contar buenas historias y a preparar ricos burritos.
—RT

Darío stared at the big red circle on the calendar. His little brother Ariel would be five years old next Thursday. Would they eat pizza and play video games? Would Ariel choose a big piñata?

Two years ago Darío had the best party at Fabulous Fiestas. All of Darío's kindergarten friends came. The outdoor play area was crazy crowded. Darío got so many presents, he couldn't even remember them. Wouldn't Ariel love a birthday like that?

Darío observó el gran círculo rojo en el calendario. Su hermanito Ariel cumpliría cinco años el próximo jueves. ¿Comerían pizza y jugarían videojuegos? ¿Escogería Ariel una piñata grande?

Darío tuvo una fiesta increíble en Fabulous Fiestas hace dos años. Fueron todos sus amigos del kínder. La zona de juegos de afuera estaba súper llena. Darío recibió tantos regalos que ni siquiera podía recordarlos todos. ¿No querría Ariel una fiesta así?

Ariel was playing with small boats on the carpet. Darío sat down beside him and said, "So, what do you want to do for your birthday?"

"I want to eat bean and cheese tacos," Ariel said.

"Is that all?" Darío couldn't believe it. "Aren't we going to Fabulous Fiestas? Don't you want to play video games? Don't you want pizza?"

"I want bean and cheese tacos," Ariel said.

"But, Ariel, don't you want to go somewhere special on your birthday?"

Ariel jugaba con barquitos en la alfombra. Darío se sentó a su lado y dijo —Y, ¿qué vas a querer hacer para tu cumpleaños?

—Quiero comer tacos de frijoles con queso —dijo Ariel.

—¿Eso es todo? —Darío no lo podía creer—. ¿No vamos a ir a Fabulous Fiestas? ¿No quieres jugar videojuegos? ¿No quieres comer pizza?

—Quiero tacos de frijoles con queso —dijo Ariel.

—Pero, Ariel, ¿no quieres ir a un lugar especial para tu cumpleaños?

"Sure. I want to go to the park." Ariel gathered all his boats together. "We can eat bean and cheese tacos at the park."

"What about a big cake?" Darío caught one boat as it slipped through Ariel's fingers. "If you don't have a cake with five candles, what will you blow out?"

—Claro. Quiero ir al parque. —Ariel juntó todos sus barquitos—. Podemos comer tacos de frijoles con queso en el parque.

—¿Y qué tal un pastel grande? —Darío atrapó un barquito que se le deslizó de los dedos a Ariel—. Si no tienes un pastel con cinco velas, ¿qué vas a soplar?

"Bubbles!" Ariel took the boat from Darío. "I'll blow bubbles at the park." He skipped towards the kitchen. "I'll tell Mom right now."

Bean and cheese tacos? Bubbles? The park? Darío thought Ariel would have the worst birthday ever!

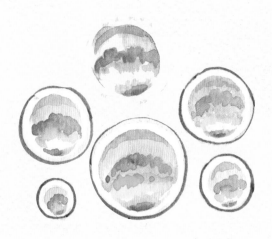

—¡Burbujas! —Ariel tomó el barquito de las manos de Darío—. Voy a soplar burbujas en el parque. —Se fue dando saltitos a la cocina—. Le voy a decir a Mamá ahorita.

¿Tacos de frijoles con queso? ¿Burbujas? ¿El parque? Darío pensó que Ariel tendría ¡el peor cumpleaños de su vida!

On his birthday, Ariel wore the kindergarten crown at lunch time in the cafeteria. Darío's second-grade friends laughed and pointed at Ariel.

Darío sighed. Ariel would be so sorry he only wanted bean and cheese tacos and bubbles.

En su cumpleaños, Ariel se puso la corona del kínder durante el almuerzo en la cafetería. Los amigos de segundo año de Darío se rieron y señalaron a Ariel.

Darío suspiró. Ariel se arrepentiría de sólo haber pedido tacos de frijoles con queso y burbujas.

After school, Darío walked over to Ariel's classroom. Usually they walked together to the daycare van for the after school program.

But today his mom stood beside Ariel waiting for Darío.

"Hey Mom, what are you doing here?" Darío asked.

"We came to pick you up for Ariel's bean and cheese taco birthday," Mom said. "Your dad's waiting in the car. Let's go to the park."

Darío grinned at his little brother. "I'm starting to like your birthday."

Después de la escuela, Darío caminó al salón de Ariel. Usualmente caminaban juntos a la van de la guardería para ir al programa de después de escuela.

Hoy su mamá estaba al lado de Ariel esperando a Darío.

—Hola Mamá, ¿qué estás haciendo aquí? —preguntó Darío.

—Vinimos por ustedes para celebrar el cumpleaños de Ariel con tacos de frijoles con queso —dijo Mamá—. Tú papá está esperando en el carro. Vámonos al parque.

Darío le sonrió a su hermanito. —Ya me está gustando tu cumpleaños.

Inside the car, Dad gave Ariel a birthday present. It was a long red boat.

"The boat has a remote control, Ariel," Dad said. "You can sail the boat all over the pond."

"What a cool present!" Darío said. If he got a boat like Ariel's, he'd always remember it.

Dentro del carro, Papá le dio un regalo de cumpleaños a Ariel. Era un bote rojo y largo.

—El bote tiene control remoto, Ariel —dijo Papá—. Puedes navegarlo por toda la laguna.

—¡Qué regalo más suave! —dijo Darío. Si a él le regalaran un bote como el de Ariel, siempre lo recordaría.

The city park had few visitors. Darío and Ariel had the best playground all to themselves. They climbed the slide and played on the swings until Mom called, "Let's eat our tacos before they get cold."

Ariel ate two bean and cheese tacos. "Delicious!"

"It's all good!" Darío exclaimed and reached for another taco.

El parque tenía pocos visitantes. Darío y Ariel tenían los mejores juegos sólo para ellos. Se subieron al tobogán y jugaron en los columpios hasta que Mamá los llamó —Vamos a comer los tacos antes de que se enfríen.

Ariel se comió dos tacos de frijoles con queso. —¡Delicioso!

—¡Todo está rico! —exclamó Darío y sacó otro taco.

Mom gave out four bubble bottles. Mom and Dad blew bubbles with each other. Darío's bubbles popped over a turtle's head peeking out of the water. Ariel blew and blew. Bubbles floated all around him.

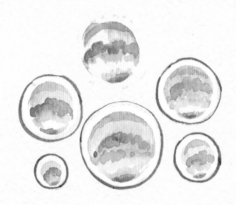

Mamá les dio cuatro botellas de burbujas. Mamá y Papá hicieron burbujas juntos. Las burbujas de Darío se reventaron sobre la cabeza de una tortuga que se asomó del agua. Ariel hizo muchas burbujas. Las burbujas flotaban a su alrededor.

As they sang "Happy Birthday," Park Ranger Salinas walked up to their picnic table. "Who's having a birthday?"

"Today my brother Ariel is five years old," Darío told him.

Ariel nodded. "Yes, here's my new boat to sail on the pond."

"Ariel," Ranger Salinas said. "For your birthday, would you like a ride in my ranger car?"

"I want my mom to come," Ariel replied, "and my brother too!"

Darío couldn't believe it! A ride in the ranger car on Ariel's birthday!

Cuando estaban cantando "Las mañanitas", el Guardabosques Salinas se acercó a su mesa. —¿Quién está cumpliendo años?

—Hoy mi hermano Ariel cumple cinco años —le dijo Darío.

Ariel asintió. —Sí, aquí está mi bote nuevo para navegarlo en la laguna.

—Ariel —dijo el Guardabosques Salinas—. Por tu cumpleaños, ¿quieres pasear en el carro del guardabosques?

—Quiero que nos acompañe mi mamá —contestó Ariel—, ¡y mi hermano también!

¡Darío no lo podía creer! ¡Un paseo en el carro del guardabosques en el cumpleaños de Ariel!

Before he started the car, Ranger Salinas turned to the back seat. "Here, Ariel, you can wear a ranger hat."

Darío laughed when the hat covered Ariel's face. Ariel pushed it up and laughed too. They waved at two old men playing checkers.

Antes de hacer andar el carro, el Guardabosques Salinas
volteó hacia el asiento trasero. —Toma, Ariel, te puedes poner
el sombrero de guardabosques.

Darío se rio cuando el sombrero le cubrió la cara a Ariel.
Ariel lo empujó hacia arriba y también se rio. Ambos saludaron
a dos señores que estaban jugando a las damas.

After the ride, Ranger Salinas showed them the life jacket, a first-aid box and the extra radios he kept in the car.

Ranger Salinas let Ariel hold one radio. He told Darío to run over to the trees with the other.

Después del paseo, el Guardabosques Salinas les mostró el
chaleco salvavidas, el botiquín de primeros auxilios y los radios
extras que guardaba en el carro.

El Guardabosques Salinas dejó que Ariel tomara un radio. Le dijo
a Darío que corriera hacia los árboles con el otro.

Darío pressed the button and said, "Ariel, your bean and cheese taco birthday is too much fun!"

Ariel's happy voice crackled over the radio. "Come on, Darío, let's go sail my boat."

Darío oprimió el botón y dijo —Ariel ¡tu cumpleaños de tacos
de frijoles con queso es muy divertido!

La voz feliz de Ariel se escuchó con interferencia. —Ándale,
Darío, vamos a navegar mi bote.

Ariel stood at the edge of the pond with the remote control. Everyone cheered as the boat sailed around the pond. Ariel's birthday smile glowed across his face. Then he turned and passed the control to Darío.

Darío felt like it had been his birthday too. He would never forget it.

"Ariel," Darío said. "Next year, I want a bean and cheese taco birthday too."

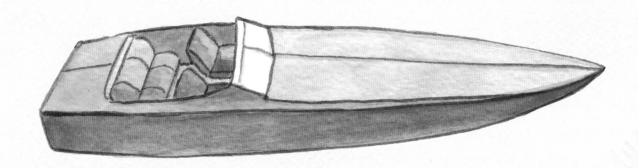

Ariel se paró a la orilla del lago con el control remoto. Todos festejaron mientras el bote navegaba en el lago. La sonrisa de cumpleaños de Ariel brilló en su cara. Luego se dio vuelta y le entregó el control a Darío.

Darío sintió como si también estuviera celebrando su cumpleaños. Jamás lo olvidaría.

—Ariel —dijo Darío—. Yo también quiero un cumpleaños de tacos de frijoles con queso para el próximo año.

Diane Gonzales Bertrand grew up in a family with five brothers. They enjoyed eating their mom's bean and cheese tacos and celebrating their birthdays together at city parks. She is the author of several picture books, including *Cecilia and Miguel Are Best Friends / Cecilia y Miguel son mejores amigos* and *Sofia and the Purple Dress / Sofia y el vestido morado*. Diane lives with her husband Nick in San Antonio, Texas. She teaches at St. Mary's University, where she is Writer-in-Residence.

Diane Gonzales Bertrand creció en una familia con cinco hermanos. A ellos les gustaba comer tacos de frijoles con queso que les preparaba su mamá y celebrar los cumpleaños juntos en los parques de la ciudad. Es autora de varios libros incluyendo *Cecilia and Miguel Are Best Friends / Cecilia y Miguel son mejores amigos* y *Sofía and the Purple Dress / Sofía y el vestido morado*. Diane vive con su esposo Nick en San Antonio, Texas. Enseña en St. Mary's University, donde es escritora en residencia.

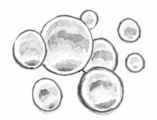

An only child, **Robert Trujillo** always wanted to share tacos with a little brother. Thankfully he was blessed with lots of cousins and a green BMX bike to fly away on. His love for picture books was inspired by his son, who loves to read and draw comics. Robert is the author and illustrator of *Furqan's First Flat Top*. He was born and raised in Oakland, California.

Como hijo único, **Robert Trujillo** siempre quiso compartir tacos con un hermanito. Afortunadamente fue bendecido con muchos primos y una bici BMX verde con la que podía volar. Su amor por los libros infantiles fue inspirado por su hijo, a quien le encanta leer y dibujar comics. Robert es autor e ilustrador de *Furqan's First Flat Top*. Nació y creció en Oakland, California.

BARRY ST. CLAIR

BUILDING LEADERS (FOR) STRATEGIC YOUTH▾MINISTRY

Previously published as
Leadership!

VICTOR BOOKS®

A DIVISION OF SCRIPTURE PRESS PUBLICATIONS INC.
USA CANADA ENGLAND

To the men and women who have shaped my leadership by their investment in my life:

Howard and Kitty St. Clair, my mom and dad, who challenged me to move beyond the limits of the possible, and supported me every time I tried it.

Buddy and Bev Price, my in-laws, who have continually modeled unconditional love and a servant attitude.

Mal and Wanda McSwain, my Young Life leaders and friends, who taught me the basics of following Christ and the essentials of youth work.

Mack Crenshaw, my spiritual leader with Campus Crusade for Christ, who demonstrated how to witness in the love and power of the Holy Spirit.

Findley Edge, my professor, who allowed me to think radically about the church.

Ken Chafin, my boss at the Baptist Home Mission Board, who encouraged my imagination and vision.

Chuck Miller, my older peer in youth ministry, who taught my the principles of strategic youth ministry.

Jack Taylor and Peter Lord, my "shepherds," who called me to deeper intimacy with Jesus Christ.

All Bible quotations, unless otherwise indicated, are from the *Holy Bible: New International Version,* © 1973, 1978, 1984 by the International Bible Society. Used by permission of Zondervan Bible Publishers. Other quotations are from *The Amplified New Testament* (AMP), © 1954, 1958 by The Lockman Foundation, and the *The New American Standard Bible* (NASB), © The Lockman Foundation 1960, 1962, 1963, 1968, 1971, 1972, 1973, 1975, 1977.

Library of Congress Catalog Card Number: 83-51683
ISBN: 0-89693-288-5

Contents

Section 2:

The Leader's Vision for Life and Ministry

Section 3:

The Leader's Knowledge and Skills for Working with Youth

Appendix

☐ INTRODUCTION

This book is designed to help you grow in three areas:
 (1) your personal relationship with Jesus Christ (section 1),
 (2) your vision for your life and ministry (section 2), and
 (3) your knowledge and skills in working with young people (section 3).
These three sections are easily adaptable to the quarterly system of most churches. Each section is designed to be used over a twelve-week period and includes eleven sessions of material and one group experience.

Section 1 of this book deals with your own spiritual life. Topics include: gaining confidence in your relationship with Christ, the characteristics of a spiritual leader, walking in the Spirit, how to spend time alone with God, Bible study, prayer, and Scripture memory.

Section 2 of this book sets a foundation for ministering to students through: developing a biblical strategy of ministry, making Jesus Lord, building a leadership team, penetrating the student culture, moving students toward maturity, and presenting Christ to students.

Section 3 of this book provides the training and practical experience involved in becoming a leader in youth ministry through: gaining a vision for your life and ministry, managing your time and gifts, leading students to Christ, helping a new Christian grow, leading a small group, counseling students, and communicating with parents and church staff.

With these purposes in mind, this book can be used for either individual or group study. On an individual level, you will spend time working through each session and making personal application of that session to specific areas of your life and ministry. As a group experience, you meet once a week with other people (called a Leadership Family) to encourage, discuss, and put into practice the things you are learning.

> The purpose of a Leadership Family is to train adult leaders of young people to be
> (1) Committed to Christ,
> (2) Committed to one another, and
> (3) Committed to ministry to students
> (See John 17:20-26.)

Here's how to get the most from your study of this book.
■ Be sure you know Jesus Christ as your Saviour and Lord. (If you're not sure, why not talk to your minister before you start?)
■ Commit yourself wholeheartedly to this experience. Expect God to do great things as a result of the time you spend working through this book.
■ Develop a stronger desire to work effectively with the students in your church or organization.
As you go through this manual, may God reward your commitment and your desire to lead students to maturity in Christ.

The Leader's Personal Relationship with Jesus Christ

SESSION 1
GETTING STARTED
(Group Project)

[This session is an informal get-together for those who plan to work their way through this book as a group. If you are not part of a group, just move ahead to Session 2.]

The goal of this session is to get to know the other people who will be studying this book with you. For the next 36 weeks you will build relationships with these people by sharing together your life in Christ. During this session, try to get beyond the "Hello. How are you?" level of conversation and really begin to open up to the other group members.

Your group leader should organize this first meeting. After some kind of opening activity, you will be asked to consider the following questions.

- Are you willing to commit your time over the next 36 weeks to complete all assignments?
- Can you faithfully attend all group meetings?
- Will you give support to the other group members during this experience?
- Are you willing to apply what you learn, both on a personal level and in reaching out to students?

After prayerful consideration of these questions, you must choose whether or not to commit yourself to your group. If you can't at this time, they will understand. It's better to drop out now than at some point halfway through the course. But if you *can* commit to this study, expect to see God do great things through you as you see yourself, and then others, grow to maturity in Christ.

NOTES:

SESSION 2
WHAT? ME, A LEADER?

Douglas Hyde is a former Communist and editor of the *London Daily Worker* who has since converted to Christianity. In his book, *Dedication and Leadership* (University of Notre Dame Press), he tells a story about a man he met after a lecture in a factory during his Communist days. The man walked up to him after his lecture and said with some difficulty, "C-c-can I b-b-become a C-c-communist?" Douglas Hyde knew well the Communist axiom: "Every man a potential Communist and every man a potential leader in Communism." But the flawed speech and unsightly demeanor of this worker took him by surprise. He told the man to return to the next week's meeting.

During the following week, Hyde's superiors mocked him unmercifully for failing to adhere to the basic axiom of Communism. They told him that this unlikely fellow could indeed become a Communist. And they were right. He did. In fact, this man who seemingly had so little potential rose to head the world literature distribution of the entire Communist Party (*Dedication and Leadership*, University of Notre Dame Press, pp. 62-69).

If you've ever wondered (with some degree of doubt and fear), *C-c-Can I b-b-become a l-l-leader of youth?* the answer is yes. *Every follower of Jesus Christ is a potential spiritual leader,* because Christians possess His life-changing power. The path to spiritual leadership parallels the path to maturity. As you commit yourself to work through these sessions, you will be challenged to mature in your relationship with Jesus Christ. And as you grow toward maturity, you will begin to recognize your own potential as a leader.

The Benefits of Leadership

As you move toward maturity and begin to sharpen your leadership skills, you will receive several benefits. You will:

- experience regular encouragement in your personal relationship with the Lord Jesus Christ.
- grow more confident in your ability to minister to others.
- discover a clearer vision for what God wants to do in your life.
- gain new skills for ministering to young people.
- develop deep friendships with fellow workers.

The Commitment to Leadership

Before you can experience the full benefits of leadership, you must commit yourself to several disciplines. Your commitment should include the following basics:

- *Set aside at least two hours to study every session.* It is not enough to read the materials. You need to give the information time to soak in and then consider ways to apply it to your specific situation.
- *Incorporate disciplines into your daily lifestyle as you are taught to do so.* You will study methods of prayer, Bible study, Scripture memory, personal witnessing, and so forth. These skills will work only if they become a regular way of life for you.
- *Develop a ministry perspective.* As you develop new skills and incorporate them into your life, the *challenge* of leadership will soon become the *privilege* of leadership.
- *Refuse to quit.* This book contains a lot of material, so determine now not to give up until you finish. One good way to keep your commitment strong is to get involved in a Leadership Family of four to eight people and work through this material together. That way you can encourage and support each other.

Right now, spend a few minutes in prayer. Consider your desire to be a better leader and the commitments you are making to yourself and to the Lord. When you are ready to move ahead, sign the Personal Commitment statement.

PERSONAL COMMITMENT

I, _____, dedicate myself to the following commitments and the growth of the young people with whom I work:

(1) To submit myself daily to Christ and learn all that He wants to teach me about growing as a Christian.

(2) To complete the assignments for every session as I work my way through the book.

(3) To be involved in my local church by supporting its regular ministry, by giving financially as God has given to me, and by ministering to its young people.

(4) To attend all group meetings unless a serious illness or circumstance prevents me (if in a Leadership Family).

I understand that these commitments are to the Lord, to myself, and possibly to my Leadership Family. I will do my best, with God's help, to completely fulfill each one.

_____
(Signature)

_____
(Date)

ACTION POINT □ Session 2

1. Refer to "Time Sheet" on page 13 to record everything you do each day this week. Be very specific. The purpose of this exercise is to evaluate your schedule in light of your commitment to develop your leadership skills.

   At the end of the week, evaluate your completed schedule. Decide on the best time for you to work on your assignments. Also, block out 20 minutes each morning for spending time alone with God.

2. After completing your schedule for the week, classify your routine activities by placing them in one of the columns below.

Activities I must do each week	Activities I want to do each week	Activities I don't need to do each week

Complete this section prayerfully. Be sure to schedule periods of free time for yourself. Avoid overcommitment.

TIME SHEET

Date

TIME	Sunday	Monday	Tuesday	Wednesday	Thursday	Friday	Saturday
6:00							
7:00							
8:00							
9:00							
10:00							
11:00							
12:00							
1:00							
2:00							
3:00							
4:00							
5:00							
6:00							
7:00							
8:00							
9:00							
10:00							
11:00							

SESSION 3
THE LEADERSHIP CRUNCH

Several years ago, a new youth minister began building relationships with some adults in his church. From those relationships, he started meeting with four young men weekly. His goal was to help them strengthen their relationships to Jesus Christ and to encourage them to become spiritual leaders. Those men continued to meet with the leader, and all four began to get involved in different areas of the church's youth ministry—evangelism (both one-to-one and in large groups), leading discipleship groups, and teaching the Bible.

Of those four men, one became a pastor, another a lawyer who works with students in his church, and one, Matt Brinkley, started his own ministry—the Fellowship of Christian Students (FCS), an organization committed to helping students grow to maturity in Christ through the local church. Ministering to students on six campuses, FCS was the result of a vision God gave Matt to involve the local church in reaching out to students.

Matt believes that he benefited from being a part of a Leadership Family because of the balanced combination of effective biblical teaching and practical application. Each time he learned a new concept of ministry, he was allowed to put it into practice in his church. He feels that the leadership principles he learned left two visible results in his church: (1) adult leaders who are mature in Jesus Christ (who continued to lead when the church did not have a full-time youth minister), and (2) spiritual depth and maturity in the students involved in the youth program (which Matt attributes to the personal ministry that the students have received from the adults of the church). Matt said, "My participation in a Leadership Family built a solid foundation in Jesus Christ for my life and ministry."

Check Your Foundation

Do *your* life and ministry have the same solid foundation in Jesus Christ? By using a parable, Jesus taught an important lesson on building foundations. Each of two builders wanted to build a house. Each had his blueprint. Each worked hard to complete his job. But there was one difference: one built his house on a rock, and the other built his on the sand.

Look at Jesus' comparison in Matthew 7. One was "a wise man who built his house on the rock. The rain came down, the streams rose, and the winds blew and beat against that house; yet it did not fall, because it had its foundation on the rock" (vv. 24-25). Can't you see this man slowly, methodically mixing the concrete that was necessary to anchor his new home to that rock? Pouring the foundation, waiting for it to dry, and making sure his work would be lasting?

But the other guy was "a foolish man who built his house on sand. The rain came down, the streams rose, and the winds blew and beat against that house, and it fell with a great crash" (vv. 26-27). Imagine his thinking, *Winter is coming, so I really need to get this house built as quickly as possible.* So he settled for sinking the walls of his house a few inches into the sand.

For a while, the second man might have sat on his balcony, construction complete, contently watching the waves roll in and out from the shore. The first man probably took longer to finish. Imagine him putting stone upon stone, carefully cementing each one to the one below.

When both houses are finished, each one is picture perfect from the outside and exquisite in every detail. But suddenly a winter storm blows in from the ocean. Imagine the utter despair of the second man as the walls of his new home topple in the sand. His investment of time and money is erased—totally wasted—in one moment of crisis.

Many times Christian leaders take the same foolish approach toward building their lives and ministries. They live in such a fast-paced world that they don't take adequate time to build their foundations in Jesus Christ. They see the overwhelming needs of people around them and quickly throw together a program filled with sports activities, fellowships, and projects. Yet all of those well-intentioned activities are only the *walls* of a structure. They make individual lives and ministries look good on the outside, but can't hold them together when difficulties come. Unfortunately, most youth ministries are like the house on the sand—they won't stand very long. Your life and ministry must be built on the solid foundation of Jesus Christ if they are to endure.

What's Important?

One way to build that strong foundation is through a Leadership Family. While the principles in this book will work on an individual basis, a Leadership Family provides for the spiritual development of adult youth leaders through small-group discipleship. As adults meet together and become committed to grow to maturity in Jesus Christ, a solid foundation for youth ministry begins to be built from within the church.

The greatest difference between the two builders in Jesus' parable, was not their vision for their work, their ability to carry it through, or their motivation to get the job done. *The greatest difference was their perspective of what was important.* One felt pressured from the immediate needs. His perspective was, "I need to get this house finished as soon as possible." The other was looking for something that would last. He wanted a building that would stand firm through each storm.

What kind of builder will you be?

ACTION POINT ☐ Session 3

1. Alan Redpath said, "It takes but a moment to make a convert; it takes a lifetime to manufacture a saint" (*The Making of A Man of God,* Revell, p. 68). What changes would you like to see in your own life? What changes would you like to see in others as a result of your ministry in their lives?

2. What are some things that might prevent you from building a solid foundation in your life or in your ministry to others?

3. Right now, pray about each of those potential problems. Ask God to give you the patience and wisdom to build your life and ministry on the solid foundation of Jesus Christ.

4. It is a challenge to allow God to bring you to maturity in Jesus Christ until you begin to exhibit the qualities of a spiritual leader. What are some goals you would like to set as you grow toward maturity? (Write them below.) Spend some time praying through your goals. Be specific. Be honest. Let God know your desires and reaffirm your commitment to allow Him to work through you to minister to others.

SESSION 4
CONFIDENT IN CHRIST

If you were asked the question, "Are you married?" you wouldn't have much trouble answering. You either *are* or you *aren't*. The same should be true about answering the question, "Are you a follower of Jesus Christ?" All it takes is a yes or a no.

Yet you might feel a twinge of uncertainty concerning your relationship to Jesus. So before we go any farther, let's make sure we're all starting at the same point. Are you a follower of Jesus Christ? Have you invited Him into your life as Lord and Saviour?

If you have made that commitment, then you have:
- admitted that you need Jesus to take away your sin and selfishness which once had separated you from God (Isa. 53:6; Rom. 3:23).
- turned away from your sins (Mark 1:15).
- given your life to Him by asking Him to take control (John 1:12).
- believed that He has come into your life as Saviour and Lord as He said He would (John 3:16; Rev. 3:20).
- begun to follow Him in obedience (John 14:15).

Can you say with confidence that each of those statements is true in your life? If not, why not remove any doubts by making a commitment to Jesus Christ right now. You can do that by acknowledging each of the above facts to God in prayer. The following prayer will help you:

Lord Jesus, I admit that I am sinful and selfish. Right now I turn from my sin. I ask You to come into my life and take control. I thank You that You are in my life. I want to obey You in everything I do. In Jesus' name, Amen.

Now read the following statements. If they are true for you, add your signature and today's date.

> I am confident that I am a Christian. Jesus Christ is in my life. I have given my life to Him, and I am now following Him in obedience.
>
> Signature: _____ Date_____

Faith, Facts, and Feelings

You can put confidence in the facts God provides. "If you confess with your mouth, 'Jesus is Lord,' and believe in your heart that God raised Him from the dead, *you will be saved*" (Rom. 10:9, author's emphasis). So your decision to ask Christ into your life should not be based on how you *feel*. Some people have an emotional experience when they receive Christ; others feel nothing at all.

Understanding the following three elements of your Christian life will prevent you from becoming confused:

Facts. The Bible is God's Word. It tells who Jesus is. It tells of His life, death, and resurrection. The *facts* about His life are the basis of our faith and feelings.

Faith. When you don't have visible proof of the facts, you can exercise your faith and be confident that what God says is true.

Feelings. Your feelings can't always be trusted. They are based on circumstances, and aren't necessarily accurate indicators of the truth. Look at the following diagram: When your faith is exercised in response to fact, your feelings will always follow.

FACT—The chair can support a person's weight.

FAITH—The chair can support my weight.

FEELINGS—Comfort and security result because an action was taken by faith based on fact.

Building a Relationship

After your initial commitment to Christ, you need to develop a daily relationship with Him. Let's explore some of the truths about your relationship with God that will affect your day-to-day walk with Him.

God created you. In fact, He created you twice! The first time, He created you *physically.* Read Psalm 139 and note the care that God put into your creation.

But God also created you *spiritually.* "We are God's workmanship, *created in Christ Jesus* to do good works, which God prepared in advance for us to do" (Eph. 2:10, author's emphasis). And we are promised that, "If anyone is *in Christ,* he is a *new creation*; the old has gone, the new has come!" (2 Cor. 5:17, author's emphasis). Romans 5:12-19 and 1 Corinthians 15:21-22 describe some of the things that have "gone" (spiritual death, condemnation for sin, the law, etc.) as well as some of the things that have "come" (God's grace, righteousness, resurrection, etc.). Right now, take time to read these passages carefully.

God cares for you. A story is told of a judge whose own son came before him in court. The judge asked his son, "How do you plead?" The son replied, "I am guilty." Because the judge was a just man, he had no choice but to sentence his son to a fine of $2,000 or a jail sentence. But when the son couldn't pay on his own, the judge as loving father stepped down from his bench, paid the fine himself, and made it possible for his son to go free.

We are not able to pay the penalty for our sin, and we stand guilty before God. But the Father proved overwhelmingly, through the sacrifice of His own Son, that He loves and cares for us. Read John 3:16-18, Romans 5:8, and 1 John 4:9-10 to see how much God cares for us.

God changes you. The presence of Jesus Christ in the lives of Peter and Paul brought about major changes in those two men. Read the following passages and contrast their lives before they knew Christ and after they committed themselves to serving Christ.

Peter before   (John 18:15-27)
Peter after   (Acts 4:13-20)
Paul before   (Acts 26:1-18; Gal. 1:13-14)
Paul after   (1 Cor. 2:1-5; Phil. 3:8-12)

After Peter and Paul changed their *individual relationships* with Jesus Christ, their lives gained purpose and power. The same is true for you! To discover how your own relationship with Christ has already changed you, compile a list of words or phrases that describe your life before and after your commitment to Christ. The following verses should help.

Before I received Christ I was:	After receiving Christ I am:
John 3:19	Romans 8:5-6
Romans 3:10-18	1 Corinthians 2:12-16
Romans 5:6	Galatians 4:4-7
1 Corinthians 2:14	Ephesians 1:3-6
Galatians 4:8	Ephesians 4:24
Ephesians 5:6	Ephesians 5:28
Colossians 1:21	Colossians 1:12-13, 22
1 Timothy 1:15	1 Peter 1:15-23
1 Peter 1:14	

If you have received Christ and committed your life to Him, the *facts* indicate that you are a special person. And even though you may not *feel* special, you can exercise your *faith* and believe it. If you've been confused about where you stand in your relationship with Jesus, review this session every day until you are truly confident in Christ.

ACTION POINT ☐ Session 4

1. Describe your "confidence in Christ." Describe how you came into a personal relationship with Jesus Christ by completing the outline below. Be very specific.

Before I met Christ:

How I met Christ:

How I have changed since knowing Christ:

2. 1 John offers several answers to the question: How do I know that I have truly become a child of God? Look up the following verses and write down the evidence that each one gives.

1 John 2:3-6

1 John 3:14, 23

1 John 3:24; 4:13

1 John 5:1

□ SESSION 5
RECEIVING GOD'S LOVE

God is the originator and source of love (1 John 4:7). He provides a never-ending supply (Jer. 31:3). Yet some people have a hard time accepting God's love because of a negative experience with human love. Somewhere along the way, their understanding of love has become either inadequate or warped. Perhaps you or some of the students you work with have difficulty comprehending and receiving the love of God. So let's try to get an accurate view of true love—God's love—and see how it surpasses human love.

Man's love is conditional. Love is not freely given. "Strings" are usually attached. "I love you if you'll take care of me," or "I love you because you act right, smell right, and look right." A condition must be met in order to receive loving feedback from most people.

God's love is unconditional. His unconditional love means that He will continue to love you no matter what you do. You don't have to earn it. God loves you in spite of your inadequacies and failures. "God demonstrates His own love for us in this: While we were still sinners, Christ died for us" (Rom. 5:8).

Man's love is stingy. It usually holds back. "I love you, but don't expect *all* my love." You can't count on stingy love when the going gets tough. If it seems to be love at all, it's only a surface kind of love.

God's love is sacrificial. Picture the cross in your mind as you read or recite John 3:16. What a sacrifice! God loves us so much that He willingly gave us His most precious asset—His Son.

Man's love is selfish. It operates on the philosophy of "You scratch my back, and I'll scratch yours." Its motive is getting, not giving (even though it may willingly give to get even more).

God's love is serving. God's love expects nothing in return. It often expresses itself through the most humbling of tasks. Jesus demonstrated such servant love when He washed His disciples' feet (John 13:1-17). He did it to show them that He loved them—not because He was getting anything out of it. Jesus is always there when you need Him. He is always willing to help you. He is never too busy to show His love for you.

Man's love is grudging. This counterfeit kind of love is evident in statements like, "I could never forgive so-and-so." A person who has been hurt by someone close (perhaps separated from loved ones through a divorce), can build up a lot of bitterness.

God's love is total. Some people think they have done things that are so bad God could never forgive them. That's not true. (See Colossians 2:13-14.) Remember His promise, "If we confess our sins, He is faithful and just and will forgive us our sins and purify us from all unrighteousness" (1 John 1:9). God's love is so complete that He will forgive us and remove all of our sin and guilt.

Man's love is limited. When someone says, "I'm going to love that person if it's the last thing I do," it is usually the last thing he does! Just when he thinks he has things under control, he blows up at that very person.

God's love is creative. As you allow it to soak in, it begins to flow through you to others. Acting on your own, you might be able to splash a drop of love here and there. But God's love going through you will flood out to others. God's love can change your life so much that you will have the capacity to love everyone (family, friends, and even enemies) in any situation (2 Cor. 5:16-17).

So if you or someone you know has had a bad experience with human love, give God a chance. His love is complete and never ending. And if you want to be a successful leader, you must radiate God's love. We'll discuss more about love and leadership in the next session.

ACTION POINT □ Session 5

1. Make a list of your *negative* experiences with love. How have those experiences interfered with your receiving God's love? Be specific.

2. Read 1 Corinthians 13. Make a list of all of the positive qualities of love, and write your own interpretation of what those qualities mean.

What love is	How it applies to me

Now make a list of the things love is not. Beside each one, write your own interpretation of what it means.

What love is not	How it applies to me

3. From this session, you may have learned that God's love is often the *exact opposite* of how people have expressed love to you. What are some of the positive qualities of God's love that counteract the negative experiences you have had?

Negative experience	·God's positive quality

4. How might experiencing more of God's love help you react to:
One specific family member?

One specific friend?

One person you find hard to love?

5. This week focus your thoughts in two areas:
   (1) God's complete love for you—unconditional, sacrificial, serving, forgiving, and creative.
   (2) Specific ways you can show the people you listed that you love them.
   Write your ideas here.

SESSION 6
A USABLE TOOL

Perhaps the greatest fear people have about becoming leaders is that they will prove to be inadequate. Have you ever felt inadequate to lead something? How did that experience turn out? Inadequacy often stems from two places: (1) a lack of preparation, or (2) the feeling that the people you are leading don't want to follow you.

At least one person in the New Testament seems to have struggled with feelings of inadequacy. Timothy was young and inexperienced during a time when wisdom and age were revered. He was also shy and timid and was probably the last person you would expect to pastor a church.

But the Apostle Paul, Timothy's "father in the faith," wrote him a letter of encouragement and instruction telling him how he should approach the task of leading his church. Here's some of Paul's advice: "The goal of this command is love, which comes from a pure heart and a good conscience and a sincere faith" (1 Tim. 1:5).

Paul seemed to be saying, "Timothy, when you lead others, lead them by loving them. And you can really love them when you have a pure heart, a good conscience, and a sincere faith."

Three Ministry Goals

Because you are a growing disciple and leader for Jesus Christ, *your* first goal in ministry should also be love. The kind of love Paul described in 1 Timothy 1:5 is *agape* love—God-given and unconditional.

Agape love will begin to flow from you when you develop a *pure heart* (a heart with unmixed motives). Like everyone else, you are susceptible to the webs of materialism, success, and pleasure. But as a spiritual leader, you need to say with the psalmist: "O God, You are my God, I seek You; my soul thirsts for You, my body longs for You, in a dry and weary land where there is no water" (Ps. 63:1).

Count Nikolaus Ludwig von Zinzendorf, an 18th-century German religious leader, put it this way: "I have but one passion. It is He. He alone." With that attitude, Zinzendorf began a prayer meeting that lasted 100 years. Hundreds of missionaries were sent out under his leadership!

Your second ministry goal should be a *good conscience*. Paul didn't challenge Timothy to do something Paul himself wasn't doing. Look at Paul's words to Felix, a Roman governor: "I strive always to keep my conscience clear before God and man" (Acts 24:16). A good conscience depends on repairing any broken relationships that may exist between you and your spouse, your family, the members of your church, or the people where you work.

My younger sister and I began to have problems when I was in high school. One day she got angry because I didn't appreciate her efforts to bring me a drink, so she dumped the drink all over the science project I was working on. I responded by slapping her. From that point, our relationship drifted apart. Years later, she told my mom what a crummy big brother I had been to her. Her accusation hurt, and God began dealing with me. Soon after that, I sat down with my sister and told her how much I really loved her. I listed every way I could think of that I had treated her wrongly, and then I asked her to forgive me. Asking her forgiveness was a humbling experience, but God used it to mend our broken relationship. The walls we had built between us came down, and the result of that experience in my life was a fresh supply of love and spiritual power flowing out through me.

The third goal of your ministry should be a *sincere faith.* This goal is important, since young people are quick to recognize hypocrisy. Put simply, a sincere faith is the result of obeying God. Someone has said, "You put into practice what you believe, and everything else is just religious talk."

Sometimes having a sincere faith seems impossible. In my own life, I have faced situations where I had to choose to do what I knew was right in God's eyes, even though the cost was high. One time I had a decision where my options were either to pay $2,500 out of my already tight budget or to break a promise I had made to someone. I chose to pay the $2,500, because I knew that price was less than the price I would have had to pay spiritually by having to live with an insincere faith.

Get Rid of Inadequate Feelings

As an adult, you are automatically a model for the students you will be ministering to. You set an example, whether you realize it or not. Young people need to see in you someone whose character consistently reflects a pure heart, a good conscience, and a sincere faith. As each of those areas of your life is more fully developed, you will experience a freedom to love others that you've never known before. And as you sense that agape love, your feelings of inadequacy will disappear.

The Apostle Paul knew that if those three ministry goals were present in Timothy's life, then it really wouldn't matter that he was young, inexperienced, or timid. As long as Timothy had a pure heart, a good conscience, and a sincere faith, God would have in His hand a usable tool—a life through which His love could pass on to others. You can also become a usable tool. The question is, *will* you?

ACTION POINT ☐ Session 6

1. Analyze the extent of each of the three ministry goals—a pure heart, a good conscience, and a sincere faith—in your own life. Pray through each of those areas thoroughly, asking the Lord to point out any area(s) that you need to improve.

2. Use this sheet to record any part of your life that you need to change. Also list any steps of action you need to take to make those changes. Then begin to take those steps *this week*. Once that is done, you can be assured that you are a usable tool in God's hand, adequate for any task He has for you. Just remember that having a "pure heart, a good conscience, and a sincere faith" is an *ongoing process* between you and God.

Ministry Goals	Steps of Action
Pure heart	
Good conscience	
Sincere faith	

SESSION 7
A LIFE FILLED UP

Dealing with frustration can be difficult. Some of life's frustrations are caused by circumstances beyond our control—pressure from job deadlines, unusual family circumstances, or stress stemming from the constant desire to measure up to other people. Other frustrations arise from saying or doing what we know is wrong.

The Apostle Paul was familiar with the problem of frustration. He said, "I do not understand what I do. For what I want to do I do not do, but what I hate I do" (Rom. 7:15). But he also discovered a key to minimizing frustration: "We know that in all things God works for the good of those who love Him, who have been called according to His purpose" (Rom. 8:28).

The secret to overcoming frustration is not found in trying to do the best we can for God, but in being totally available to God so He can do His work in us (being "called according to His purpose"). But how can we develop the desire to allow God to work through us?

Gaining the Desire

Before you became a Christian, *you* were responsible for your life—making decisions, reacting to situations, and carrying all of the weight that accompanies responsibility. There wasn't anything wrong with that then, since you were all you had to count on.

But one of the basic truths of your faith in Jesus Christ is that *He* has now taken responsibility for you. His death on the cross paved the way for you to have a "father-child" relationship with God (Rom. 8:15). That kind of relationship is one of dependency. Gaining the desire for what is right begins with understanding *your need to have God as the one who directs your life.*

"Trust in the Lord with all your heart and lean not on your own understanding; in all your ways acknowledge Him, and He will make your paths straight" (Prov. 3:5-6). As you begin to *trust* God because of what Jesus did on the cross, you will begin to live in a relationship of healthy dependency on Him.

While Jesus' death made possible a new relationship with God, Jesus' resurrection makes possible a new life—one of submission to Him. Now you have an inward source of power (the Holy Spirit) to help you make right decisions and react properly to situations. The ability to overcome the frustration of doing what you know is wrong comes when you learn to tap into your source of power.

Gaining the Power

Tapping into the Holy Spirit's power source requires a clear channel of communication between you and God. This communication is achieved by: (1) confessing your sins to God (1 John 1:9), and (2) claiming that Christ is in control of your life (Eph. 5:18). You must then keep that channel clear on a day-to-day basis.

A good illustration of communication with God is the physical process of breathing. Hopefully you've been breathing since before this session started, even though breathing is something you really don't think a lot about. It's automatic. You breathe out impurities from your lungs, and then breathe in life-giving oxygen.

Spiritual "breathing" serves a similar purpose in your walk with God. When you *exhale* (by confessing your sins to God), you become pure. When you *inhale* (by claiming Christ's control of your life), you are given strength to live the kind of life God has called you to live. Spiritual breathing should be no less important to us than physical breathing.

Ephesians 5:18 tells us: "Do not get drunk on wine. . . . Instead, be filled with the Spirit." Right now, ask the Spirit to fill you. You might want to use a prayer similar to this one: "Lord Jesus, I confess my sin to You. (Name the specific sin.) I ask You to fill me with Your Holy Spirit now." Then repeat this prayer daily as you practice spiritual breathing.

The Greek word used for "fill" literally means "to wholly take possession of the mind." So to be filled by the Spirit means to be completely under His influence. Being *filled* with the Holy Spirit means we are to be *controlled* by the Holy Spirit.

After you've tapped into the power source provided by the Holy Spirit, then what? How can the power of God *within* you be transformed into *outward* signs of God's presence in your daily life? The Apostle Paul wrote, "Live [walk] by the Spirit, and you will not gratify the desires of the sinful nature" (Gal. 5:16).

Releasing the Power

Notice that "Walk by the Spirit" is a command. Therefore, it follows that the Holy Spirit's control does not happen to us automatically. We must choose to live under the influence of the Spirit on a day-to-day basis. Walking by the Spirit is something that we decide to do *from now on.*

We must meet certain conditions before we can continually be filled with the Spirit. They are:

(1) *Do not grieve the Holy Spirit* (Eph. 4:30). We grieve the Spirit by yielding to anything that is opposed to Him. If lusts, passions, or evil desires are controlling us, we cannot be controlled by the Spirit. Any Christian who lives a life of sin grieves the Spirit.

(2) *Do not quench the Holy Spirit* (1 Thes. 5:19, NASB). Another Bible version translates it this way: "Do not put out the Spirit's fire" (NIV). The Holy Spirit within is stimulating us, giving us ideas, producing thoughts, and making suggestions (John 14:26). Every time I refuse to act on those thoughts, I am

not letting the Spirit control me. Therefore, I "quench" His power.

(3) *Realize that the Holy Spirit is within you* (1 Cor. 6:19). It is usually because we forget that the Spirit is within us that we are not controlled by Him. As we yield to Him and desire His fellowship, we will continue to consult Him, acknowledge His presence, and ask Him to manifest Himself more and more to us.

Carefully heed the Holy Spirit's promptings. Those promptings are His way of leading and guiding you. Wait for Him, expect His help, and listen to Him. Don't shortcut His leading.

REMEMBER: Walking in the Spirit and overcoming frustration involves:

- *Understanding* your need for God's direction in your life.
- *Clearing* the channel of communication you have with Him by confessing your sins and claiming Christ's forgiveness and control of your life.
- *Being filled* with the Holy Spirit by *not* quenching or grieving Him, but by realizing that He lives in you and desires your fellowship and obedience.

ACTION POINT □ Session 7

1. What frustrations do you face in:
   your job?

   your family?

   your friends?

   yourself?

   As you look back over your list, have any of your frustrations been caused or aggravated by your own wrong attitudes or actions?

2. Have you asked the Holy Spirit to fill you? How can you practice spiritual breathing every day?

3. Under each category below, write your own personal evaluation of how well you are doing in that area of your spiritual life.

   Not grieving the Spirit

   Not quenching the Spirit

   Realizing the presence of the Spirit

☐ SESSION 8
FEEDING YOURSELF

Imagine you are in an all-you-can-eat smorgasbord restaurant—one that has every kind of food imaginable. You are hungry and *everything* looks good, so you walk around and analyze the food. The tomatoes are full of potassium. The steak has plenty of protein. The macaroni is high in carbohydrates. The oranges can provide the daily requirement of vitamin C. The bread and cereal are full of fiber.

But looking at the food won't remove your hunger. You can study it, write reports about it, and even have seminars and discussions about it. But if that's *all* you do, you will *starve to death.*

Maybe that's a ridiculous illustration, but it's an exact description of what is happening (in a spiritual sense) to many people in the church. The spiritual food they need is available in abundance, but all they do is discuss and analyze it and remain spiritually starved. How can someone who is continually hungry think about feeding someone else?

Colossians 2:6-10 describes how you can be spiritually full. Notice the phrase in verse 10: "You have been given fullness in Christ." But how can you come to "fullness" in Christ? To better understand the passage, picture a banquet table loaded with all kinds of delicious food. The food represents the fullness that Christ has to offer. But before you can receive any of the food, you must take some practical steps.

Step #1—Walk to the table. Paul told the Colossian church, "Just as you received Christ Jesus as Lord, continue to *live* in Him" (Col. 2:6). Some translators use the word *walk* in that verse instead of "live." The meaning is similar, but *walk* indicates a specific action to take.

When you walk toward someone, you are planning to meet that person and build your relationship. Jesus Christ desires that you experience His fullness. In order to do that, you must walk *to* His table.

Step #2—Be seated at the table. Paul writes that we are to be "rooted and built up by Him, strengthened in the faith as you were taught, and overflowing with thankfulness" (Col. 2:7). When a person becomes "dead serious" about eating, he not only walks to the table, but also makes sure he is *firmly entrenched.* Look at the words Paul used to describe this process:

Rooted—Why do the roots of a tree run deep into the ground? For *nourishment.*

Built up—After nourishment, a tree grows (is built up) and becomes *strong.*

Established—When a tree becomes strong after nourishment, it will be established and it will not be blown down when the storms come. The same is true in the life of a Christian. When you become firmly entrenched at God's table, you will have nourishment and strength, and you will not be blown away by the storms of life.

George Mueller, a 19th-century pastor known for his work with teenage orphans in England, once confessed: "I see more clearly than ever that the first great and primary business to which I ought to attend to every day is not how much I might serve the Lord . . . but how I might get my soul into a happy state, and how the inner life might be nourished."

When you are seated at God's table to receive His fullness, you are provided with utensils to help you eat the food. It is not that you can't get by without them, but eating is much more pleasant when you use the utensils. Four utensils are provided:

■ Prayer (Eph. 3:20-21)
■ The Word (Jer. 15:16)
■ Fellowship (Heb. 10:25)
■ Witnessing (Acts 1:8)

Each utensil, when used properly, will help you better enjoy "the feast" Jesus Christ provides as you come to fullness of life in Him.

Step #3—Be careful what you eat. "See to it that no one takes you captive through hollow and deceptive philosophy, which depends on human tradition and the basic principles of the world rather than on Christ" (Col. 2:8). One paraphrase of that verse might be: "Don't let what you are supposed to eat, eat you!" When you eat the wrong food, one of two things will happen (or maybe both):

(1) You will not receive the proper nourishment, or
(2) you will get an upset stomach.

Paul suggests four sources to the Colossian church that are more likely to provide spiritual indigestion than nourishment:

■ Intellectual, secular philosophy—In Paul's day, a group of people tried to present the Gospel so that only "intellectuals" could understand it. In a later letter to Timothy, Paul offers advice to help his young disciple overcome the problem of such incorrect philosophies. He told Timothy, "Do your best to present yourself to God as one approved, a workman who does not need to be ashamed and who correctly handles the word of truth" (2 Tim. 2:15).

■ Empty deceit—In our world, empty deceit poses as the "good life." Men seek wealth, pleasure, comfort, happiness, power, prestige, and other "empty" things that don't really satisfy. But the Scripture tells us to "Seek first His kingdom and His righteousness, and all these things will be given to you as well" (Matt. 6:33).

■ Traditions—Someone has aptly said that the seven last words of the church will be, "We've never done it that way before." Healthy traditions are fine, but for some people, church and religion turn into nothing more than going through the motions. The key to avoiding unhealthy traditions is to *ask God for fresh food every day!* We can be as sure as the Children of Israel in the wilderness that God will provide fresh "manna" every morning.

■ Legalistic do's and don'ts—Many people see Christianity as "Don't drink, don't smoke, don't chew; don't hang around with people who do." A legalistic dependency on the "basic principles of this world" prevents us from experiencing *real* nourishment that God wants to provide for us.

Now that you have walked to the table, seated yourself, discovered what utensils you have, and become aware of what food *not* to eat, you can *feast* on Jesus Christ! He will bring you to *fullness* of life in Him.

TO GET PROPER SPIRITUAL NOURISHMENT, REMEMBER:
■ Don't analyze the food.
■ Don't get sidetracked.
■ Use the utensils of prayer, God's Word, fellowship, and witnessing to *nourish yourself in Jesus Christ!*

ACTION POINT ☐ Session 8

1. Work through the following "Survey for Growing Disciples."
   Rate yourself on a scale of 1 (definite yes) to 5 (definite no)
   in relation to the statements below.

SURVEY FOR GROWING DISCIPLES

	YES 1	2	3	4	NO 5
I have absolute assurance and security concerning my salvation (1 John 5:11-13).					
I often experience God's total love and forgiveness (Eph. 1:7).					
I know what it means to be Spirit-filled and I am able to consistently walk in the Spirit (Eph. 5:18).					
My prayer life is regular, spontaneous, and consists of praise, confessions, thanksgivings, petitions, and intercessions. I see God answer my prayers (Eph. 6:18).					
I am growing in my knowledge of who God the Father and Jesus the Son are, and what place they have in my life (Eph. 1:3).					
I regularly hear the Bible taught and preached (Rom. 10:14).					
I read from God's Word regularly and have a definite program to study the Bible (1 Tim. 4:13).					
I know how to study God's Word (2 Tim. 2:15).					
I have a regular and consistent method of memorizing and reviewing Scripture (Col. 3:16).					
I enjoy meditating on Scripture and find my thought patterns changing and the Word becoming more real to me (Eph. 4:22-24).					
As I learn God's Word, I form convictions that influence my beliefs and actions (2 Tim. 4:2).					

2. After completing this session on feeding yourself and taking the "Survey for Growing Disciples," what is one area of weakness you have discovered in your life? What is one action you need to take in order to get rid of that weakness and come to the table to receive the fullness of Jesus Christ?

3. Review the goals you set for this study in the *Action Point* section of session 3 (question #4). In what way(s) do you need to reevaluate those goals in light of what you have already studied?

☐ SESSION 9
SPENDING TIME ALONE WITH GOD

Think back to your first date. Did it go something like this?

A guy, sweaty hands and all, finally gets enough of a grip on himself (and the telephone receiver) to dial the number. After only three wrong numbers his nervous fingers dial the correct combination. He has wanted to ask the girl out for weeks. On the other end, she almost faints at the sound of his voice, because she has been waiting for him to ask her out for months.

Then come all of the details. Where will they go? What time? How will they get there? What are they going to talk about? All of these are important questions, but number one on the list is: Will they really like each other? Everything hinges on that basic relationship.

Human relationships usually develop gradually and follow a pattern:

- you are attracted to someone
- you get to know the other person better
- you establish a loving, caring relationship with that person

You move from one step to the next by spending time with that person. The same is true in your relationship with God. One of the secrets of all growing, dynamic Christians is that they consistently spend time alone with God.

At what stage is *your* relationship with God? Do you spend time alone with God every day? Do you spend time alone with God on a regular basis? Are you getting to know Him more and more? Have you already developed a deep love relationship with God? Would you like to learn how to have a consistent time alone with God?

Remember all of those details from your first date? Going through the same kind of detailed planning for your time alone with God will help your relationship with Him grow quickly. Below are some areas you need to consider.

Choose a time. Schedule a regular time to meet with the Lord every day. A good time to meet is first thing in the morning. Have you ever watched an orchestra warm up *after* a concert? Or a team put together their game plan *after* the game? Having an early time with God will prepare you to face the day. Jesus often met with the Father in the morning (Mark 1:35), and He is a good example to follow. After a few weeks, check to make sure the time you have set is still the best time for you.

Choose a place. Find somewhere that is quiet and conducive to your being able to talk with God aloud. Get away from your normal surroundings so you won't be distracted or interrupted. Abraham talked to God in the desert, Moses on the mountaintop, and Daniel in the quiet of his room. Wherever you meet with God will become a special place for you.

Choose to prepare. Your mental attitude is important as you meet with God. Prepare to come to God quietly and reverently, but also rested and alert. Psalm 46:10 provides some good advice: "Be still, and know that I am God."

Here are other ways you can be prepared for your time with God:

- *Look to Jesus.* Instead of worrying about the details of your day or the bad things that could happen, let your first thoughts focus on Jesus.
- *Keep a Time Alone with God notebook.* Record your thoughts, prayer requests, answers to prayer, Bible study notes, and insights God gives you each day. You will soon have an unbeatable source of inspiration as you look back to see how many things God has been doing in your life.
- *Don't give up.* If you miss your time with God one morning, don't worry about it. Just try your best not to miss the next day.
- *Be honest.* If you feel that your time with God is empty and worthless, tell Him so. But don't quit. Ask God to increase your desire to meet with Him.
- *Be consistent.* Some of your times with God will be wonderfully insightful. Others will be very routine. The way you *feel* is not always an accurate indicator of success. Every day that you spend time alone with the Lord will strengthen your relationship with Him, even if you don't sense the results right away.

Your ultimate goal for spending time alone with God should be to know Him better—not to become a whiz at Bible study or set a record for verses memorized or prayer hours logged. Bible study, Scripture memory, and prayer are all important, but they are only steps to achieving your main goal of developing a deep love relationship with the Lord. Set your sights on Jesus, and the other spiritual benefits will come naturally.

ACTION POINT ☐ Session 9

1. The whole concept of "building a relationship" suggests action. Read the following verses and write down *actions* you can take to build your relationship with God:
Matthew 6:33

Philippians 3:10

Matthew 22:36-38

2. Read the following verses to discover some of the goals God has for your life:
1 Corinthians 10:31

Jeremiah 33:3

Philippians 4:6-7

How do you think that spending time alone with God each day will help those goals become realities in your life?

3. Right now, choose a time to be alone with God for 20 minutes every day to read Scripture and talk with God in prayer. Be open to hearing what He wants to say to you during those times. (You may feel a little awkward at first, but soon this will become a special time for you.) Write the time and place you choose here.

Also begin a Time Alone with God notebook if you haven't yet done so. (If you put *Time Alone with God Notebook Inserts* in a 5¹/₂″ X 8¹/₂″ binder, you'll have everything you need to get started. You may photocopy the *Inserts* from pages 133-141 of this book.)

SESSION 10
PERSONAL BIBLE STUDY

Imagine going to (or think back to) your ten-year high school reunion. Of all the things you might expect to experience, the biggest surprise is probably your recognition of how things *change*. (This fact is evident from the expanding waistlines and receding hairlines all around you.)

Suppose one of your friends, whom you haven't seen since high school, approaches and tells you about his terrific job, his loving family, and his large house. Then he turns to you and asks, "Do you feel like *you've* been successful over these past ten years?" How would you answer him? Why?

God's plan for success is written in Psalm 1:1-3. A vital element of "success" from God's point of view is "delighting in the law of the Lord." In other words, a successful person gets excited about spending time in the Word of God.

Why should you spend time in God's Word? And how can time alone with God make you successful? Take a look at the following reasons.

You will get to know yourself better. As you spend time in God's Word, you will begin to see it penetrate your life. Like a skillful surgeon who uses his scalpel to carefully remove threatening cancerous growths, God uses His Word to remove the things that keep us from becoming all He wants us to. "The Word of God is living and active. Sharper than any double-edged sword, it penetrates even to dividing soul and spirit, joints and marrow; it judges the thoughts and attitudes of the heart" (Heb. 4:12).

You will get to know Jesus better. The more you read the Word, the more you will understand Jesus—His life, His death, and His resurrection. "These are the Scriptures that testify about Me" (John 5:39).

You will grow as a Christian. In a prayer for His disciples, Jesus said: "Sanctify them by the truth; Your word is truth" (John 17:17). *Sanctify* means "to grow into all God wants you to be." But just knowing that God's Word is the truth will not automatically help you grow as a Christian. Peter tells us to *crave* good spiritual milk (1 Peter 2:2). Just as babies need milk to help them grow into healthy adults, Christians need God's Word to help them mature into men and women of God.

You will have a successful life. When a person meditates on God's Word daily, he will be "planted"—like a tree. According to Psalm 1:3, three things will happen to him: (1) He will yield fruit in season; (2) His leaf will not wither; and (3) Whatever he does will prosper.

You will be able to handle temptation. Bible study gives you the ammunition to handle any situation the way Jesus would.

As you spend time in God's Word, He will direct you to passages such as 1 Corinthians 10:13: "No temptation has seized you except what is common to man and God is faithful; He will not let you be tempted beyond what you can bear. But when you are tempted, He will also provide a way out that you can stand up under it."

The following hints will help you in your Bible study:

■ Stick to the time you've chosen to meet with God.
■ Study the Bible for personal meaning, not for how it applies to others.
■ Be willing to let the Holy Spirit change you.
■ Record your insights from Scripture each day.

Remember: The Bible is not just literature to be studied or facts to be learned. It is truth to be applied.

ACTION POINT □ Session 10

1. How would you evaluate your knowledge of Scripture?
   _____ Well-developed. I enjoy the Bible and apply its teachings with ease.
   _____ Getting there. I feel like I'm growing daily in my knowledge and application of Scripture.
   _____ Almost nonexistent. I just can't seem to get excited about studying the Bible.

2. Use a Bible Response Sheet (from your *Time Alone with God Notebook Inserts*) to do a Bible study on Psalm 1:1-3. If you need help understanding how to use a Bible Response Sheet, refer to this completed one (on John 1:1-5).

3. Continue to have a time alone with God each day, spending 15 minutes in Bible study and 5 minutes in prayer. Use the Book of Mark for your Bible readings. Just read a few verses each day and then work through the Bible Response Sheet to help you assimilate the material you have read. Suggested readings for the first week are below. The entire Book of Mark is broken down into suggested daily readings on the Check-Off Sheet in the Appendix (p. 132).

   Day 1: Mark 1:1-3
   Day 2: Mark 1:4-8
   Day 3: Mark 1:9-13
   Day 4: Mark 1:14-15
   Day 5: Mark 1:16-20
   Day 6: Mark 1:21-26
   Day 7: Mark 1:27-28

BIBLE RESPONSE SHEET

DATE _5/10_

PASSAGE _John 1:1-5_

TITLE _Jesus brings light + life_

KEY VERSE _verse 4_

SUMMARY _the Word (Jesus)_
(1) was in the beginning,
(2) was with God, (3) was
God, (4) made all things,
(5) was life, and (6) was
light

PERSONAL APPLICATION _I need to let_
Jesus be who He wants to be
to me. I can experience His
life + light by spending 15
minutes alone with Him every
morning for the rest of this
series of studies.

SESSION 11
MEMORIZING SCRIPTURE

It's a Saturday night and you've gotten comfortable watching your favorite TV show. During one of the commercials you joyfully discover that the late-late show is one you've been wanting to see, so you settle down for a fitting finish to a nice evening. You even stay up to watch the national anthem. But on your way to bed you happen to see a corner of your Sunday School quarterly sticking out from under a copy of *Sports Illustrated*, and you suddenly recall that you haven't prepared your lesson for tomorrow.

You grab your Bible, diligently begin searching for some gems to share with your class, and everything begins to fit together. *No problem,* you think as you finish your notes, say a quick prayer, and then turn in for the night.

The next morning you oversleep and get to Sunday School just in time for the opening prayer. As you check out the crowd, you see that *every one* of your students is present. You even have a few visitors.

After the preliminary activities, you open up your Bible and quarterly and begin to teach. But the notes you took last night don't seem to make sense anymore. Your mind goes blank, because you *know* the material, but you just can't *recall* it. You struggle through the notes you prepared and then look at your watch—a whopping ten minutes have passed. As you look into the bewildered faces of your students, you realize you have forty minutes to go before the bell rings. And you can't think of a thing to say.

Sound familiar? All of us have faced situations where we weren't as prepared as we should have been. We've studied (sort of), but we just can't remember what we've learned when we really need it. The same thing is often true when it comes to learning the Bible.

It's good to read the Bible. It's even better to study it carefully. But if you stop there, you won't be any more ready for the emergencies of life than the Sunday School teacher in the opening illustration. The Word of God needs to be readily accessible to you at all times.

During biblical times, Jewish men wore phylacteries—small leather boxes containing verses of Scripture that were tied to the left arm and between their eyebrows—when they prayed. These men *literally* carried God's Word with them.

But you can carry God's Word with you with no boxes or strings attached. Scripture memory allows you to carry God's Word with you all the time! We are instructed to "Bind them [God's Words] upon your heart forever" so that "When you walk, they will guide you; when you sleep, they will watch over you; when you awake, they will speak to you" (Prov. 6:21-22).

Benefits of Scripture Memory

Memorizing Scripture will benefit you in a number of ways.

The Bible will come alive for you. Read Psalm 19:7-10 to discover a few benefits of God's Word. Among other things, God's Word:

- Revives your soul (v. 7)
- Is a source of truth and wisdom (v. 7)
- Is a source of joy and enlightenment (v. 8)
- Endures forever (v. 9)
- Is always righteous (v. 9)

You will gain strength to face everyday situations. Obviously, most people can't study the Bible all day long. But when you carry its teachings in your mind and heart, you can recall those truths during spare moments or at other times when you really need them. God's Word is called the "sword of the Spirit" (Eph. 6:17). It's your weapon to fight the battle. Scripture memory allows you to carry your weapon with you at all times.

You will prosper spiritually. In the last session we saw that a person who delights in the "law of the Lord" (God's Word) is like "a tree planted by streams of water, which yields its fruit in season and whose leaf does not wither" (Ps. 1:2-3). Hiding God's Word in your heart will help you become firmly rooted in your day-to-day walk with Jesus Christ.

You will have strength to overcome temptation. Take a close look at these words from Psalm 119:9-11: "How can a young man keep his way pure? By living according to Your Word. I seek You with all my heart; do not let me stray from Your commands. I have hidden Your Word in my heart that I might not sin against You." When a person memorizes Scripture, he has the ability to overcome temptation.

You will be a witness for Jesus Christ. When you "hide God's Word" in your heart, you will always be ready when He gives you the opportunity to speak for Him. Like David, you can "recount all the laws that come from [God's] mouth" (Ps. 119:13). Many people feel that they don't know what to say when they witness for Christ. But after you have memorized Scripture, you always have something to say.

You will begin to see things from God's perspective. When God's Word becomes an integral part of your life, you begin to think the way God thinks. This is what Paul had in mind when he said to "be transformed by the renewing of your mind" (Rom. 12:2).

In spite of the many benefits of Scripture memory, you might be thinking, *It's no use. It sounds good, but I have a lousy memory.* Before you give up, try this simple experiment: What's your name? Your address? The names of your family members? Your telephone number?

Your memory is probably better than you think. If you can

learn dates for special meetings or directions to friends' houses, then your memory can't be all that bad. You can be sure that you will find a way to remember *anything* that is of personal interest to you. Your attitude affects your memory.

Adopting an attitude of *confidence* and *desire* will help you learn to memorize Scripture. David summed up this type of attitude when he said, "Because I love Your commands more than gold, more than pure gold, and because I consider all Your precepts right, I hate every wrong path. Your statutes are wonderful; therefore I obey them" (Ps. 119:127-129). As you develop a stronger love for God's Word and a desire to hide it in your heart, you will experience the many benefits that result from the rewarding practice of Scripture memory.

ACTION POINT ☐ Session 11

1. What are some of your obstacles to Scripture memory?

3. List the reasons why you *can* memorize Scriptures.

2. What are some positive reasons to memorize God's Word?

4. Memorize 2 Timothy 3:16. Before you start, refer to the section in your *Time Alone with God Notebook Inserts* labeled "How to Memorize Scripture." After you memorize a verse, review it each day as you learn new ones. *The Key to Scripture memory is review.*

5. Continue spending time alone with God each day this week, with 15 minutes in Bible study (the Book of Mark) and 5 minutes in prayer.

SESSION 12
A PROPER UNDERSTANDING OF PRAYER

It's 6 A.M. Your alarm rings and your first impulse is to catch another hour's sleep before you begin the day. But you've promised God this is the day that you will start getting up earlier in order to spend more time with Him. It would be a lot easier to spend time at the Church of the Inner Spring (mattress, that is) under the warm protection of the Reverend Sheets. But you figure your snoring isn't what the psalmist meant when he said to "make a joyful noise."

So how do you convince yourself to get up and keep your commitment to the Lord? The key is to *have a proper understanding of prayer.* Some people think of prayer as a chore, much like taking out the garbage. It's something they don't really enjoy, but they do it anyway to keep the air clean. But prayer should be more like dialing the combination that unlocks a safe. It should open up all of God's riches for you. When you don't understand the purpose of prayer and consequently fail to pray, that door remains shut.

The Purpose of Prayer

Prayer exposes you to who God is, what He wants you to do, and how He wants you to do it. Through prayer you learn to converse with God on a personal level. You begin to understand His will for you. Soon you discover that you have the power—His power—to do whatever He asks you to do. In fact, Jesus promised that, "You may ask Me for anything in My name, and I will do it" (John 14:14).

Douglas Thornton was a student who saw the positive effect that spending time in prayer was having on some of his classmates. He had a lot of trouble getting up in the morning, but was determined to begin each day in prayer. He finally built a device from a fishing pole, four hooks, and an alarm clock. When his alarm rang in the morning, the pole would be released to pull on the four hooks, which were attached to the four corners of his sheet. Once the covers were pulled off the bed, it wasn't so hard for him to get up.

That method might sound a little extreme. That is, it might sound extreme until you consider the question: "How much did Douglas Thornton want to know God?" His desire to know God was so strong that he risked looking foolish in order to spend time in prayer every day.

Maybe you've made past commitments to pray more often, only to forget. Perhaps you don't have a real desire to pray. Your commitment should be a result of your motivation (desire) to meet with God. If you have no inner desire to meet with Him, you're much less likely to honor your commitment to Him. But if you really want to know God better, you'll find some way to spend time in prayer with Him daily.

God's Answers to Prayer

Sometimes people don't pray because they don't understand the way God answers prayer. They pray for something, seem to get no answer, become discouraged, and quit. But God can respond to our prayers in several different ways.

When you ask for something according to God's will, His answer will always be yes. How can you be sure? Remember the promise found in John 14:14: We may ask *anything in Jesus' name* (according to His will) and He will do it.

When you pray with a double mind, the answer will always be no. You cannot pray something contrary to God's will and expect Him to answer you affirmatively. James writes about those who doubt when they pray: "That man should not think he will receive anything from the Lord; he is a double-minded man, unstable in all he does" (James 1:7-8).

God's answers to our prayers also depend on *His perfect timing.* Sometimes God says "Wait" before He says "Yes." One possible reason is for you to build your faith by persevering in prayer.

As you develop a consistent prayer life, God will teach you to discern His will. Then you will be able to pray according to His desires.

Different Aspects of Prayer

Prayer involves more than just making requests of God. There are at least *five* aspects of prayer. Each aspect is a part of your communication with God that will help you get to know Him better and better.

Praise may be the single most important ingredient in prayer. It is an open response of your love for God. Through praise you express back to God the qualities that are true of Him, and you adore Him for who He is. Praise also helps you handle fear. When you praise God in a fearful situation, you recognize His ability to handle every problem. And after you begin to see your problem from His perspective, it doesn't seem so threatening.

Thanksgiving reveals a heart of gratitude. It shows an awareness for what God has done, expresses appreciation for His works, and honors His actions and gifts. If you know what God is really like, you can thank Him for *every* circumstance—good or bad, difficult or easy, exciting or mundane.

Confession removes any barriers sin might have put between you and God. Your confession shows that you *agree* with God that you have done wrong and that you *accept* the forgiveness that Jesus' death has provided for you.

Petition is asking God for what you need. He wants you to have good things. In fact, God is the source of *every* good gift

(James 1:17). Petition is the key that unlocks God's storehouse of those riches for you.

Intercession releases the power of God's Spirit in the world. You are to be an "ambassador" (2 Cor. 5:20) and pray for specific individuals and circumstances. You make known specific needs to God, and in turn, He releases His Holy Spirit to deal with each particular situation.

Each of these aspects of prayer is a vital part of building your relationship with God so you can get to know Him on a deeper level. The more you pray, the better you will understand and love God. At the same time, through consistent prayer you will experience His love and concern for you as you see Him answer your prayers.

ACTION POINT ☐ Session 12

1. Read Matthew 18:18-20 and John 14:12-14. What do you discover about prayer from these passages?

2. Think of one prayer request in your past when God said yes, one when He said no, and one when He said to wait. Be specific. Looking back, can you see why He answered those prayers the way He did?

3. God's Word provides hundreds of promises pertaining to prayer. But His promises won't mean much to you if you don't apply them to specific situations in your life. Look up the following passages and discover how they apply to you personally. Then begin to claim them during your times alone with God.
Matthew 7:7-8

Philippians 4:6-7

Philippians 4:19

James 1:5

4. Spend a few minutes evaluating your prayertime with God. How can it be improved? What can you do to make those improvements? What obstacles have been keeping you from praying "wholeheartedly"?

5. Memorize John 15:7 this week.

6. Begin to fill out a Prayer Action sheet each day during your time alone with God. A reproducible form is in the *Time Alone with God Notebook Inserts,* as well as daily Scriptures you can use for each section (praise, confession, thanksgiving, petition, and intercession). One example of a completed Prayer Action Sheet is shown here.

PRAYER ACTION SHEET

Date **5/10**

PRAISE:
Write down one reason to praise the Lord today.
His majesty and His magnificent creation (Psalm 8)

THANKSGIVING:
Write down what you are most thankful for today.
my new job

CONFESSION:
Write down any sin(s) you need to confess.
I have been having impure thoughts, and I want to see others as Christ would.
Write down a promise you can claim.
Phil. 4:8 – I can think about things that are true, noble, right, pure, lovely, and admirable.

PETITION:
Write down any needs you have in your life today.
I need God's grace to help me be able to apologize to John at work.

INTERCESSION:
Write the names of the people you are praying for today and a phrase that expresses your prayer for each person.

Name	Prayer
Karen	*help with family problems*
our pastor	*wisdom for the future*

Important reminder: Make sure you have completed all assignments from Section 1 (daily times alone with God, memory verses, and weekly studies and projects) before moving on to Section 2.

From now on, you should fill out one Bible Response Sheet and one Prayer Action Sheet each day. Spend about 12 minutes in Bible study (continue in the Book of Mark) and 8 minutes in prayer.

The Leader's Vision for Life and Ministry

☐ SESSION 13
A HALF DAY OF PRAYER
(Group Project)

[This session is designed as a group project, but the benefits of prayer are just as rewarding on an individual level. If you aren't part of a group, why not read through this session and plan a half day of prayer on your own before moving ahead to Session 14?]

An organized half day of prayer can be a special learning experience as you are given the opportunity to apply everything you have covered so far. The outline below should get you started in the right direction. Add any specific needs or activities that you wish.

Step #1: Orientation (10 minutes)

Meet together to discuss the schedule, collect any materials you have prepared, and ask questions you may have.

Step #2: Individual prayer (3 hours and 20 minutes)

Go to an area where you can be by yourself to spend individual time alone with God. Gauge your time in order to cover three major areas:

■ Waiting on the Lord—Realizing His presence, being cleansed, and worshiping Him.
■ Prayer for Others—Making specific intercession for the needs of other people.
■ Prayer for Yourself—Petitioning God openly and honestly about your own needs.

Vary your activities during each of these areas. You can pray a while (both aloud and silently), read the Scriptures, plan and organize, or whatever else is relevant to this special time alone with God. Be sure to list the requests you take to God, so you can follow up on them in future prayertimes.

Step #3: Response (30 minutes)

Reassemble as a group so each person can share what he learned or observed about himself or God through this experience.

MATERIALS NEEDED:

ESSENTIAL	HELPFUL	OTHER OPTIONS
Bible	Missionary prayer letters	Calendar for the year ahead
Time Alone with God Notebook	Sack lunch/ beverage	List of personal goals/objectives
Pen	Memory Cards	List of personal decisions to be made
Clock or watch	Devotional/Prayer books	Songbook

☐ NOTES:

SESSION 14
DEVELOPING A BIBLICAL STRATEGY

The guy was popular, a member of the football team, and going steady. But over a period of time, he began to party and use some drugs. Then he and his girlfriend got careless and she got pregnant. They both left town. Several months later, the young man returns alone and wants you to help him. As he tells you his story, you begin to wonder: "How do I begin to minister to this young man?"

What you need is something that will help this young man (and the many other students you know) begin to move in a positive direction with his life. If he is going to experience healing of the hurts and wrong choices he has already made, he needs to experience a relationship with a loving and forgiving Saviour. And if he is going to reach the point where he can make good, sound decisions, then you also need a plan that will help him grow to maturity.

This particular troubled student happened to meet a youth worker who knew how to minister to him. That youth worker began to build a relationship with him and invited him to a meeting at his church. During that meeting, the young man was presented with the Gospel and turned to Christ. The youth worker then guided him into a small group of other students who were studying about Jesus Christ and what it means to be a Christian. With teaching and encouragement, the young man began to grow. Today, after completing a degree in counseling and finishing seminary, he is working with students who are like he was when he was in school. Beautifully, miraculously, one young man met Jesus Christ, grew to maturity in Him, and is now leading others to Jesus Christ.

If the same troubled student had shown up at your church or organization looking for help, would you be prepared to help him? If your answer is no or if you aren't sure, you need to develop a *strategy* for ministering to young people. The following chart illustrates what is called the Reach Out Strategy.

REACH OUT STRATEGY

UNDER THE LORDSHIP OF JESUS CHRIST

The Big Event: A youth group rally geared toward students' need and providing students the opportunity to receive Christ.

Adult-to-Student

Leadership Family: Adult youth workers becoming equipped to minister to students and help them grow to maturity in Jesus Christ.

Adult-to-Student

Touch Ministry: Adults spending regular time with young people at school and other student activities in order to build relationships with non-Christian students.

Student-to-Student

Adult-to-Student

Student-to-Student

Discipleship Ministry: Small groups of students who meet regularly (with an adult) to help each other grow toward maturity.

The five basic elements of the Reach Out Strategy are described below in a little more detail:

The Lordship of Jesus—This is essential in the life of every youth worker. You can only take students as far as you have gone yourself. As you submit to Christ's lordship, you will continue to grow in your own relationship with Him. Your personal relationship with Christ will speak louder to students about *their* relationships with Jesus Christ than anything else you can say.

The Leadership Family—Equipping youth workers in the church is crucial. A youth worker needs proper training and encouragement in order to grow personally and help students know Christ and grow in Him. The Leadership Family provides that training for the people who will be working with youth.

The Touch Ministry—The youth worker must move beyond the walls of his church and go to places where students spend their time. When youth workers begin going to campuses and getting involved in student activities, they become available to students. Students are more willing to talk about Jesus Christ when they know somebody cares about other areas of their lives too.

The Discipleship Ministry—While many youth groups lack interest in spiritual things, the groups that have discipleship ministries are usually characterized by spiritual depth. Discipleship is the key to spiritual growth. The student "disciple" learns to develop his relationship with Jesus Christ by spending quality time with his discipleship group and in a one-to-one relationship with the group's leader.

The Big Event—This part of the Reach Out Strategy is the culmination of all the other elements. When your Leadership Family is meeting and then spending time with students on campus (in Touch Ministries), and when your young people are participating in discipleship groups, you can effectively minister to non-Christian students. Both the Leadership Family and the discipleship groups bring their friends for an exciting meeting during which secular students are exposed to the truths of Jesus Christ and given an opportunity to receive Jesus as their personal Saviour and Lord.

In future sessions you will study each of the five elements of the Reach Out Strategy in more detail. Pray that God will help you begin to develop a personal strategy that will result in a life-changing ministry to students.

ACTION POINT ☐ Session 14

1. Read through the first four chapters of Mark and examine Jesus' strategy of ministry. Pick out specific verses that support each element of the Reach Out Strategy.

Lordship of Jesus:

Leadership Family:

Touch Ministry:

Discipleship Ministry:

Joy Explosion:

2. Evaluate the involvement of your church or organization according to the Reach Out Strategy guidelines. Beside each element, write down what you are currently doing with the strategy and what you would like to do in the future.

	Now	**Future**
Lordship of Jesus		
Leadership Family		
Touch Ministry		
Discipleship Ministry		
Joy Explosion		

3. Picture in your mind the following images and write one name (from your youth group) beside each description:

A 9th-grade cheerleader

A kid in trouble

An athlete

An average person in your youth group

Now picture each person you listed as he or she might be five years from now. Write a brief prediction of each person's future.

NAME	PREDICTION

4. What can you and your church do to help each person you listed become like the student at the beginning of this session—one who comes to know Jesus, matures, and is fruitful and motivated as a Christian? Describe what you feel needs to happen and why.

What I need to do

What my church/organization needs to do

5. Memorize Mark 1:17 and continue your daily readings from the Book of Mark.

☐ SESSION 15
MAKING JESUS LORD, Part 1

Think back to the first day you started a new job. How did you feel? Could you do everything you needed to do right away? Did someone train you? How long did it take you to "get in the groove"?

Learning to live as a Christian takes time too. You need to be trained by someone who knows what he is doing. Jesus is your "teacher" for the Christian walk. When He becomes Lord of your life, your heart's desire will be to obey and please Him more than anyone else.

But before you can make Jesus Lord, you need to respect Him. Is He worthy of your respect? Let's examine His credentials to be Lord of your life.

Credential #1—*He created you.* Jesus is the Living Word of God. Read John 1:1-18 substituting "Jesus Christ" each time "the Word" is used. Compare that passage in John to Colossians 1:15-16. Jesus Christ was involved in the whole process of the creation of the world, and more specifically, in *your* creation.

Because He created you, Jesus knows how you function best. Read Psalm 139:13-16. Jesus Christ knows *everything* about you. His unsurpassed knowledge of you qualifies Him to be your Lord.

Credential #2—*He identifies with you.* Picture in your mind a story where a young fearless prince delivers his country from an evil ruler. Jesus lived that story (as the hero). He "gave Himself for our sins to rescue us from the present evil age, according to the will of our God and Father" (Gal. 1:4).

Jesus Christ came to earth as a man. Through His death, He crushed Satan's rule on this earth forever. Since Jesus lived here for 33 years, He knows the problems and temptations we face every day. "We do not have a High Priest who is unable to sympathize with our weaknesses, but we have one who has been tempted in every way, just as we are" (Heb. 4:15). Jesus deserves to be your Lord because He faced the same problems you face, yet remained sinless.

Credential #3—*He redeemed you. Redeem* means to "rescue" or "ransom." Another definition for *redeem* is to "recover ownership by paying a specified sum." Jesus has legally obtained ownership of your life. He has the right to be your Lord because He has bought you. "You are not your own; you were bought with a price" (1 Cor. 6:19-20).

So Jesus has the credentials to be Lord of your life. Just what should that mean to you? It depends on your definition of "lord." There are three Greek words in the New Testament that describe Jesus as our Lord. Let's look at each word and its English equivalent.

Despotes (master)—The meaning here is "someone with unlimited power." Jesus can master any situation because His power has no limit.

Basileus (monarch)—This word is more commonly used to indicate someone with "all power and authority." A monarch's word is law, so Jesus is superior to other monarchs because His word is always truthful and right. His authority is the final authority.

Kurios (lord)—A lord of something, in this sense of the word, is the owner. *Kurios* indicates authority, but also conveys a feeling of wisdom and love. Jesus is the wise and loving owner of your life.

The Apostle Paul summarizes what God has done as a result of Jesus' death, burial, and resurrection: "God exalted Him [Jesus] to the highest place and gave Him the name that is above every name, that at the name of Jesus every knee should bow, in heaven and on earth and under the earth, and every tongue confess that Jesus Christ is Lord, to the glory of God the Father" (Phil. 2:9-11).

Jesus deserves to be your Lord. He has the credentials and has been given authority from God to rule in your life. The question you must answer is simple: *Do I respect Jesus enough to go ahead and submit to His lordship in my life?* Your response to that question determines your ability to lead others. Give it some serious thought before you continue.

ACTION POINT ☐ Session 15

1. Look back at the three different definitions for the word *lord*. Then write your own definition of "lord."

2. You can do two things right now to prepare you to have Jesus as Lord of your life. First, you need to develop *desire*. The psalmist wrote: "O God, You are my God, earnestly I seek You; my soul thirsts for You, my body longs for You, in a dry and weary land where there is no water" (Ps. 63:1). How do you create that degree of desire? One way is to get desperate! When you get tired of running your life on your own, you will become willing to allow God to do it His way. Are you desperate? Another way to create desire is to focus on Jesus. The more you see who He really is, the more desire you will have to please and worship Him. Right now, assess your desire for Jesus. Be honest.

What facts do you already know about Jesus that can encourage you to turn your life over to His lordship?

After desiring Christ's lordship, you must *decide* to let Him be Lord. When Paul, on the road to Damascus, realized who Jesus really was, he said: "What shall I do, Lord?" Jesus said to him, "Get up and go into Damascus. There you will be told all that you have been assigned to." What did Paul do? He went into Damascus. His decision to obey nailed down his commitment to Jesus as Lord of his life (Acts 22). What steps of obedience do *you* need to take that will lead to Jesus' lordship in your life?

Begin to take those steps right now by faith. Realize that Jesus will make your desire for His lordship greater and greater as you continue to walk with Him. And He will honor your decision for obedience. After you commit yourself to serve Jesus as your Lord, fill in the statement below.

Today, _____, I took the following
             (Date)
steps of obedience in response to Jesus' lordship:

_____

_____

_____

_____
        (Signature)

Writing down your commitment will be a source of encouragement to you later on.

3. Finally, to encourage you in the lordship of Jesus, memorize Philippians 2:9-11.

SESSION 16
MAKING JESUS LORD, Part 2

Every New Year's Eve people make lists of resolutions that usually include one group of bad habits they intend to give up and another group of good habits they plan to begin. But those good plans and intentions are usually forgotten by mid-January. Making Jesus Lord is more than a fading resolution—it is a lifetime commitment.

Jesus calls you to excellence in your walk with Him, whether it is New Year's Eve or not. Making Jesus Lord means facing life-changing decisions. What will it cost you to make *that* kind of resolution? Let's take an honest look.

Paying the Price

Read Matthew 16:24-26. Jesus uses some strong statements to describe His expectations for His disciples. He is asking you to be willing to lose your life for Him. How can you do that?

Losing your life involves forgetting yourself. Several translations of Matthew 16:24-26 use the phrase "deny yourself." That means you must replace your self-centeredness and personal ambition with a sold-out commitment to Jesus Christ. The world says to "look out for number one." But Jesus says you can forget yourself because He has taken responsibility for looking out for you. You don't have to worry (or even think) about your own life! Jesus also knows that when you are preoccupied with your own self-interests, those things (not Jesus) will motivate you.

Losing your life involves carrying your cross. Paul gives us a good picture of a person who carried a cross. In the last session you studied and memorized Philippians 2:9-11 to see how God exalted Jesus. But Philippians 2:5-8 describes what Jesus had to do before He was exalted. Jesus took up (and died on) His cross as an obedient servant of His Father. You carry *your* cross by being willing to give up anything that doesn't serve your Master and by enduring suffering. Jesus endured the pain of the cross. Suffering is the spiritual equivalent of the pain you go through to get your body into shape physically. The pain and pressure eventually produce good results.

Losing your life involves following Jesus. Following Jesus means you should be His companion in a relationship with Him. It also means that you agree with Jesus' goals for your life and are willing to submit to His direction in your life.

Receiving the Benefits

Forgetting yourself, carrying your cross, and following Jesus will be the personal costs to you if you are going to make Jesus Lord of your life. But you will also receive many benefits as a result of having Jesus as your Lord.

You will make the best decisions. When Jesus is Lord of your life, you are in the center of God's will for you. As a result, when you have tough decisions to make, God will give you specific guidance (Prov. 3:5-6).

You will find satisfaction. Think about how your mouth feels when you are really thirsty. Jesus is your spiritual "thirst quencher" (John 4:10-14). Do you need satisfaction right now? Jesus is a "river of life" flowing out of you. He satisfies every need you have.

You will be a winner. Jesus makes us victorious in life and victorious over death. "Thanks be to God! He gives us the victory through our Lord Jesus Christ" (1 Cor. 15:57). When Jesus is your Lord, you share in that ultimate victory!

Your character will change. "We know that in all things God works for the good of those who love Him, who have been called according to His purpose. For those God foreknew He also predestined to be conformed to the likeness of His Son, that He might be the firstborn among many brothers" (Rom. 8:28-29). Being "called according to His purpose" is another way of saying "He is Lord of my life." "Conformed to the likeness of His Son" means you will have Jesus' character expressed through your life.

Your future will have hope. Many things can make life tough these days: losing a loved one, being disliked because of your convictions, being out of work, etc. No matter how bad things might look right now, you have a bright future! If you remain faithful during your tough times, a time will come when you will reign with Jesus (2 Tim. 2:11-12).

Don't forget Matthew 16:24-26. Whoever *loses* his life will *find* it. Jim Elliott, a missionary who was killed by Auca Indians in 1955, said it this way: "He is no fool who gives what he cannot keep to gain what he cannot lose" (*Shadow of the Almighty,* Elizabeth Elliott, Harper and Row).

Think of it this way: You give Jesus the blank sheet of your life, and He gives you back a blank check. You let Him write on your blank sheet of paper whatever He desires for your life. In return, you can use His blank check to claim promise after promise of His provision for you (Rom. 8:32; Eph. 1:3; and 2 Peter 1:3, to name a few).

So even if this isn't New Year's Eve, are you willing to make a resolution to give Jesus all of you—laying down your life to experience your full potential in Him?

ACTION POINT ☐ Session 16

1. Study Romans 12:1-2. Look for practical steps for making Jesus Lord that relate to you personally. List them below.

2. Romans 12:1-2 also has the answer to how you can stop "looking out for number one." When Paul says to "offer your bodies," he means that you should place your mind, feelings, and desires (as well as your physical body) at Jesus' disposal. The phrase, "as a living sacrifice," refers to dying to those areas where you are still putting yourself before God. Spend at least 30 minutes reflecting over some specific ways that you are still "looking out for number one." Consider the following areas.

Your thoughts (2 Tim. 2:22; Matt. 5:27-28)
Do you read books and magazines or attend movies that stimulate impure thoughts? Do you let your mind turn to lustful thoughts of the opposite sex?

Your relationships (Matt. 5:23-24; 6:12-14)
List the people with whom you have a wrong relationship. Do you hold a grudge toward anyone? Do you have a good relationship with your parents, spouse, children, and other family members?

Your attitudes (Eph. 4:31-32)
Is there anyone toward whom you have a bad attitude? Do you complain? Gripe? Criticize?

Your desires (Matt. 6:33; Col. 3:9-10)
Do you put too much emphasis on material possessions (clothes, cars, making money)? Do you lie, steal, or cheat?

Your physical body (1 Cor. 6:19-20)
Are you careless with your body? Do you have habits which defile your body?

3. Spend time in prayer concerning your response to question #2. Remember that as you "die to self," God will give you His very best in return.

4. Read and study Philippians 2:3-11. You have the mind of Christ within you. What can He do in you to transform *your* thoughts, relationships, attitudes, desires, and physical body into *His* thoughts, relationships, attitudes, desires, and what He wants for your physical body? Write down one positive step that you need to take in each area.

Which step do you need to take first?

Will you take it now?

5. Memorize Matthew 16:24 and continue your daily quiet time in the Book of Mark.

☐ SESSION 17
BECOMING A LEADER, Part 1

In working with young people, do you ever wonder, "Why am I doing this?" Check the activities below that sometimes frustrate you as you work with students.

_____ Serving cookies and Kool-Aid after meetings.

_____ Keeping students out of the bushes on church retreats.

_____ Driving on youth outings with music so loud the windows could blow out at any minute.

_____ Cooking on retreats or picnics without one person saying "Thanks."

_____ Teaching Sunday School for students who don't want to be there.

_____ Leading a rowdy youth group on Sunday nights.

_____ Songleading when the kids don't sing.

_____ Attending meetings where nothing happens.

Have you ever thought to yourself, _There has to be more to youth work than what I am experiencing?_ If so, you are right where you need to be. Leadership involves more than being a cook, a Kool-Aid server, or a bus driver. Each of those activities is important, but none of them takes the place of your becoming a spiritual leader in your church's youth ministry.

Webster defines _leadership_ as the "ability to show the way or guide the course of action of another by going before or going beside." As you examine that definition, one thing becomes apparent about being a leader. You can't show someone else the way to go unless you have been there (or are going there) yourself. In other words, _the quality of your life will determine the quantity of your influence._ As you minister to students, you must catch hold of the concept that, "If I take care of the depth of my spiritual life, then God will take care of the breadth of my ministry." Simply stated, _leadership is a lifestyle._ God can use you to influence others, but your influence will be in proportion to the type of lifestyle that you lead.

Jesus had a very definite leadership lifestyle. His approach to ministry contained four steps: (1) I do it; (2) I do it and my students are with me; (3) My students do it, and I am with them; and (4) My students do it and I am in the background to encourage. We'll examine the first two steps in this session and the other two in the next session.

I Do It

Jesus said, "I always do what pleases Him [God the Father]"

(John 8:29). Jesus was completely committed to do everything God asked Him to do. In order for you to effectively lead others, you need the same kind of relationship with God.

Your lifestyle needs to be one that you want others to follow. If you are not spending time alone with God each day, memorizing Scripture, sharing your faith, or showing love toward others, you can't expect those things from those you lead. As you become more and more committed to doing things that please God the Father, you become a godly model for others to follow. Paul was confident enough in his own relationship with God to say to others, "Follow my example" (1 Cor. 11:1). You can be just as confident as long as you are being obedient to what God asks of you.

I Do It, and My Students Are with Me

Take a minute to read John 13:1-10. These verses show Jesus as a man who was willing, not only to be with His disciples and serve them, but also to show them, with real transparency, who He was. Through everyday situations, He demonstrated His vulnerability to His disciples. Others will learn the _most_ when they see us apply what we teach to our own lives in everyday situations.

The importance of being "transparent" became evident to me as I was discipling a high school student named Kent. I had asked Kent to help me move some couches in my house. When we pulled the first couch out from the wall, we discovered all sorts of junk that had fallen behind it (with the help of my three kids)—a wash rag, some moldy raisins, various toys, and other junk. I looked over at Kent, and I just knew he was thinking, _Sloppy, really sloppy._

We went downstairs to get a hide-a-bed to put where the first couch had been. After we got it in place, we opened it and a wad of stuffing as big as a pillow dropped out onto the floor. Kent stood there with an embarrassed, sheepish grin on his face. I could tell he was thinking, _What a cheap couch._

Well, we had one more couch to move, but this time we ran into some logistical problems. This couch was 80″ × 35″ and the doorway we were trying to go through must have been 79″ × 29″. We pushed, we shoved, we sweated, and we got pinched fingers. Moving that couch turned into a long-term project—it took several days before we finally figured out how to get it through the doorway. Needless to say, by the time we were through, Kent had seen me struggle. He had watched me live life as it really is. He began to see me as a person with not only strengths and talents, but also flaws and weaknesses.

When we are bringing someone alongside us in the Christian walk, a natural tendency is to try and cover up anything that indicates we don't have everything under control. But false perfectionism only leads the person following us to think, _I could never be like that._ As a result, he becomes totally frustrated with his own walk with Jesus Christ. On the other hand, when we are open and honest (transparent), then the person can say, "Hey, I can identify with that!"

We need to let the people who follow us see us in life situations. Then we realize what Paul meant by, "I will boast all the more gladly about my weakness" (2 Cor. 12:9). Paul knew, and we can discover, that God's *strength* is made perfect in our *weakness.*

Leadership is a lifestyle—your lifestyle—of commitment to Jesus Christ. When you show a willingness to allow others to see that commitment with its strengths *and* weaknesses, you will be the kind of leader who leaves a lasting impact on the lives of others.

ACTION POINT ☐ Session 17

1. Prior to reading this session, what would you have listed as your top three responsibilities as a youth leader? Would you change your list as a result of reading this session?

2. Study John 13:1-10. What style of leadership does Jesus portray? Why is Jesus' example significant to us as we lead others?

3. What are some things you do that provide a godly model for others to follow? Are you to the point in your spiritual life where you can tell students to "Follow my example"?

4. What activities do you normally do alone where you could begin to include some of your students? List at least three.

5. How do you feel about becoming a "transparent" model for your students to follow? What steps can you take to ease any fears you may have?

6. Memorize 2 Corinthians 12:9 and continue your daily times alone with God in Mark.

SESSION 18
BECOMING A LEADER, Part 2

Think about a leadership experience from your past when you felt like no one was following. Obviously, leadership is not supposed to be that way. When you lead, people should follow. As you begin to apply the two principles you studied in the last session, students will listen to you because your lifestyle will make them desire what you have. As you develop friendships with students, they will want to hear what you have to say. The first two leadership principles—"I do it" and "I do it and my students are with me"—help young people learn how to have a growing relationship with Jesus Christ through your personal example. In the next two leadership principles, the focus changes from setting the example to helping your students become examples themselves.

Someone once said: "You can catch a fish and feed a person for a day, or you can teach a person how to fish and feed him for a lifetime." Jesus taught His disciples how to feed themselves spiritually. This is clearly shown in His next two principles of leadership: "My students do it, and I am with them" and "My students do it, and I am in the background to encourage."

My Students Do It, and I Am with Them

After Jesus' disciples had seen Him minister, the time came for them to minister on their own. He first sent out the 72 disciples in pairs "like lambs among wolves" to go ahead of Him and tell about His coming (Luke 10:1-3). Jesus was never far away, in case they needed Him. He was giving them firsthand experience at doing the things He had taught them. He wanted the truths and skills He had taught them to become cemented in their hearts so they would begin to apply those truths daily. He provided them with on the job training.

My Students Do It, and I Am in the Background to Encourage

In the three years that they were with Him, Jesus' disciples experienced the miracles that Jesus performed—healing the sick, casting out demons, etc. Then they saw themselves performing those miracles with Jesus' authority. They also faced the great disappointment of the cross.

The disciples experienced real life with Jesus, but one final step needed to be taken before Jesus' ministry in their lives was completed. As Jesus ascended to heaven, He promised the disciples that His Spirit would come to empower and motivate them (Luke 24:48-49; Acts 1:8). Then He commissioned them to complete His ministry on earth through the power of the Holy Spirit (Matt. 28:18-20). Jesus moved from His role as direct overseer of His disciples into the background. The ministry that was to take place would from that point take place through His disciples.

The Leader As a Motivator

As you begin to apply these last two principles in your ministry to students, here are several points to take into consideration:

During the stage of "My students do it and I am with them," *you* are the motivator. After showing them *what* to do, you must provide the opportunity for them to learn *how* to do it. For example, you teach them how to spend time alone with God. Then you challenge them to spend time alone with God for the next week. Then a week later you discuss what they learned by spending time alone with God. Then you challenge them to spend time alone with God for the next 14 days. Then you discuss it again and again until you see your students being motivated to spend time alone with God on their own.

During the phase of "My students do it, and I am in the background to encourage," your disciples are inwardly motivated about their relationship with God. They continue to spend time alone with God without having to be told. They take the initiative to put into action what you have taught them.

Don't move from "I am with them" to the "I am in the background" level until your students show you through their actions and attitudes that they are capable of staying motivated in various areas of their walks with the Lord.

To summarize, being an effective leader involves:

Principle #1   Exhibiting a lifestyle that others will want to follow

Principle #2   Developing open relationships with your students so they can see how you react in everyday situations

Principle #3   Creating an environment where they can develop and strengthen their relationships with Christ

Principle #4   Continuing to teach them until they are spirit-motivated to live a consistent Christian lifestyle.

Looking to the Future

You will know that your job as a leader in discipling someone else has been successful when you see these things evident in the lives of your student disciples:

■ Desire for a quiet time—not because they have to, but because they want to

■ Scripture memorization for personal growth, not just because it is assigned

■ Genuine concern for others

■ Desire to take leadership in the group

In my own life, I have felt no greater joy than that of watching God use me to lead another person to the point where he can lead others. What a privilege! What a challenge!

ACTION POINT ☐ Session 18

1. Using a Bible and a concordance, trace Peter's growth as a leader. Begin in the Gospels when Christ first called him and follow his growth to Acts 2 where 3,000 people were converted after he preached. (Look up the references in your concordance under "Peter.") Write your own outline below.

2. From your study of the life of Peter, respond to the following questions.

   What was Peter doing before he met and followed Jesus?

   What leadership skills and training did Peter learn from Jesus?

   When did Peter become inwardly motivated to be a leader?

3. In what areas of your own relationship with Jesus Christ do you feel inwardly motivated to be a leader? In what areas of leadership do you struggle and still feel you need some outward motivation?

4. Reflect on the four principles of Jesus' leadership style and Peter's growth in leadership development. Then write out what you think is an accurate description of *your* leadership style. Be specific.

5. Take a minute to think about the students in your youth group. Is there one in particular with whom you would like to begin developing a more open friendship? Who is it? Right now, stop and pray that God will give a good opportunity to do so. If God were to allow you to lead that person, how would you go about it? (Think back over the things that you have learned during these last two sessions.)

6. Memorize 1 Thessalonians 2:19 and continue your daily Bible readings from the Book of Mark.

SESSION 19
PENETRATING THE STUDENT CULTURE, Part 1

Think back to your days in high school. Make a mental list of the things that were popular. What clothes were in? What was *the* car to drive? What music did you listen to? What did you do on Friday nights? What kind of parties did you have? What constituted a "hot date"? Now answer these same questions about your life as it is today. How has life changed since your high school days?

Face it. You have changed! But you aren't the only one. Walk down the hall at your local high school and you'll notice that student culture has changed as much as you have. Different hair styles. Different clothes. Different cars. Different values.

But the basic needs of students remain the same. What are some of those needs? And how can we begin to meet them?

The Needs of Students

Students need *heroes*. Does that somehow sound unspiritual? Or juvenile? It really is not. Students are beginning to develop their own personal value systems and lifestyles. They look around to find people whom they consider successful, sharp, and content with life. Young people want to pattern their lives after these "heroes."

Students need love. More specifically, they need role models of loving relationships. According to statistics, the average family spends less than 38 minutes each week in meaningful conversation. Such a lack of communication suggests to students that they are not important. Many students live with only one parent and miss out on having a full and rich relationship with the other. And many young people from two-parent families rarely detect a loving relationship between their father and mother. As a result, many students have no idea what real love is.

Students need hope. Many students today realize the truth of Proverbs 13:12: "Hope deferred makes the heart sick." High school campuses are filled with young people who feel like they have been let down by their family, their friends, and life itself. Some try to escape through drugs, sex, or suicide. Only Jesus Christ can give them a hope that "does not disappoint" (Rom. 5:5).

Students need purpose. They are searching for answers to nagging questions like "Who am I?" and "Why am I here?" The answers aren't easy. Students need to hear that they have a better option than "just getting by." They need to know that

lasting purpose can be found in Jesus Christ. Only when they come "to know Christ and the power of His resurrection" (Phil. 3:10) will they understand that they have been created for a specific purpose.

When facing similar needs, Jesus said, "The harvest is plentiful but the workers are few. Ask the Lord of the harvest, therefore, to send out workers into His harvest field" (Matt. 9:37-38). Jesus' exhortation has never been truer than it is today concerning the student culture. Students are becoming more open to change than ever before. This session will examine one exciting way that He can "send out workers" into the ripe fields of today's students. The method is called the Touch Ministry.

Building Strong Relationships

The Touch Ministry puts us as adults in touch with secular students so we can build relationships. Then out of those relationships we begin to introduce students to abundant life in Jesus Christ. The key to building strong relationships that meet students' needs is to go where they are.

It takes a special kind of individual to go where students are. The people who participate in the Touch Ministry need to begin with the following characteristics.

A desire to be with young people (Luke 15:1-2; John 1:14). If you want to reach students, you must move out of the secure, comfortable environment of the adult world into the world of the school campus and the local hangouts. After visiting a high school campus, one layman said, "The thought of going into their territory was a little overwhelming. When you think of how many unsaved students there are, it can be a little scary when you begin wondering if they'll accept or reject you. But when I got there I realized the impact we could have on students' lives. I was very encouraged at how well I was received by my own church's students. Their smiles told me how much it meant to them and how encouraging it was for them to have one of their youth leaders on their turf. I was surprised how many new relationships could be built by just being on campus."

A desire to win the friendship of young people (1 Thes. 2:8). Spending time with students is the key to building friendships. Teenagers spell love, T-I-M-E. As you show concern for them as individuals and try to learn what their interests and needs are, your friendships with students will deepen. As one youth leader said, "The Touch Ministry gives us credibility with the students who are outside of our church. If the only time they see us is on Sunday, it is easy for them to think that we don't understand what's going on in their lives and therefore don't care about them. Our being on campus makes students feel like they are important to us. They're right. They *are* important!"

A desire to see young people come to know Jesus (Matt. 4:19). Availability and sensitivity to the needs of young people eventually provide the opportunity to share Christ openly, boldly, and lovingly. As one leader put it, "Nothing is quite as exciting as sitting down with a student one to one and telling him about Jesus Christ and then helping him ask Jesus into his life."

A desire to learn to love students right where they are (Luke 5:12-16). Students today have a tremendous need for love. Try not to be scared by their actions, angry at their rebellion, or frustrated by their apathy. Students are crying out through their behavior for real relationships. Being involved in a Touch Ministry gives you the opportunity to work through your own feelings toward students and begin to really love them. One youth minister sums it up this way: "As a result of being part of a Touch Ministry, I feel a great compassion toward students. What they really need is love, encouragement, and someone who has a solution to their problems."

Take a few minutes to think about the students you are working with in your youth ministry. Pray that God will give you His love for them. What are some unique talents and gifts that you possess that will help you relate to students? Ask God to show you how you can begin to use those gifts and talents to minister to students.

ACTION POINT □ Session 19

1. What are some characteristics of student culture that you have recently observed?

What do you see in Jesus' approach to people that demonstrated His care for them?

2. Who are some people you could reach through a Touch Ministry?

4. What can you learn from this passage about ministering to students?

3. Read Luke 5:12-16. What qualities did Jesus have that caused Him to touch the man in spite of his sickness?

5. Do you feel like you have the basic desire needed to participate in a Touch Ministry? Why or why not?

6. Memorize Matthew 9:37-38. Continue your daily time alone with God and readings in Mark.

SESSION 20
PENETRATING THE STUDENT CULTURE, Part 2

The Apostle John gave us a perfect cure for overcoming any fears about stepping into the student culture: perfect love. "Perfect love drives out fear" (1 John 4:18). John's statement has two different applications. First, your love for Christ will motivate you to do whatever is necessary to bring students to Him. Second, as you get to know the students in your area, you will grow to love them so much that you will soon feel very much at home with them. Below are some tips that will help you "get in gear" as you approach a Touch Ministry.

■ *Pray.* Because Christ lives in you, you can do anything! (Phil. 4:13) Jesus is the One who helps you overcome the initial fear of going on campus. Claim His promises and provision for you, and pray that God will give you His peace about meeting new students (Phil. 4:6-7).

■ *Think agressively.* Your first reaction to a Touch Ministry on campus may be, "That's not part of my personality." But as Christians, we are all "fishers of men" (Matt. 4:19). A fisherman does not expect the fish to jump into his boat. He goes where the fish are and aggressively tries to get them into his net. That's why you need to go where students are. *Fearless youth workers are needed to "go fishing" for students!*

■ *Get involved.* Jesus had no fear of sinners. He talked with them and He ate with them. As you get involved with students, it is amazing how your fears will disappear. Just focus on their needs instead of fears.

■ *Identify with students.* The greatest act of identification took place when Jesus came to earth as a man so He could reveal God to us (John 1:14). In the same way, you need to identify with the hurts, problems, joys, and triumphs that students experience so you can reveal Jesus to them.

■ *Respond with sensitivity.* Jesus had a phenomenal ability to sense the needs of individuals. Students may need the healing touch of a hug, a pat on the back, a shoulder to cry on, or someone they can count on. You can be that kind of friend to them.

■ *Go with confidence.* As a minister, Paul saw himself as God's representative—whether or not other people saw him that way (2 Cor. 5:20). He knew who he was and where he was going. Students may not always understand what you are doing, but as Christ's ambassador *you* will know that God sent you.

■ *Care about people.* Paul spent time investing his life in other people. He loved others as a mother loves her baby. He said that he gave people not only the Gospel, but also his very own life (1 Thes. 2:7-8). As you work with students, nothing will be more important than having caring relationships with them.

Getting Started

Once you begin to practice these principles with students, you will find that your fears melt away into real love for students. So how do you begin a Touch Ministry with students?

Step #1—*Get permission to visit.* Set up an appointment with the school principal to explain who you are and what you want to do. (Go with your youth minister, if you have one.) Offer to help any way you can because you care about students and want to help them. This approach opens the door. Making requests or demands doesn't go over very well, even for a worthy cause like a Bible study or an assembly.

Even if your school is closed to off-campus visitors, a Touch Ministry can still work for you. Look for creative alternatives concerning student activities *outside* of school (football practice, drill team rehearsal, students walking home, local hangouts, ball games, choir practice, drama rehearsals, etc.). You can usually find some way to meet students where they are.

Step #2—*Select the best time for you.* You can usually choose from several good times each day to get involved. Some suggestions are:

■ Before school—Give students rides to school. Walk with them to class. Spend time meeting new students in the halls before classes start.

■ During lunch—Eat with students in the school cafeteria. If a Touch Ministry is new for you, make an appointment to eat with one young person from your church. This will give you a good reason to go.

■ Extracurricular activities—Participate by becoming a club sponsor, a coach for a school sport, a chaplain of a team, etc. Attend games, matches, meets, plays, and other school functions.

■ After school/evenings—Become a "regular" at the local hangouts and spend time with students there.

Step #3—*Surround your Touch Ministry with prayer.* Pray before, during, and after the times that you are to be with students. Prayer not only helps alleviate your fears. It also gives God an opportunity to prepare you to face specific students or problems.

Step #4—*Continue to meet new students.* The tendency is to stick with the students you know and like. Don't fall into this trap. Discipline yourself to spend time with different groups and meet new people on a regular basis.

Step #5—*Don't push for school time or facilities.* The temptation is to start out trying to get a room for devotions or a Christian club, or to request a time for an assembly. Resist the temptation. First build a trust relationship with the adults at the school. Then later you may have earned the right to begin these other activities. And always have a reason for being on campus. Do not go when school is in session except by permission of the administration or for special occasions such as assemblies, pep rallies, and other events open to the public.

In a Touch Ministry, remember the following basics:
- Look for ways to serve students.
- Play no favorites.
- Practice learning names.
- Be yourself.
- Have a sense of humor without being insulting.
- Be available.

Your goal in a Touch Ministry is to build relationships, not to promote the church. *Make it your policy not to share Christ on campus, but to wait until you can be in a neutral setting.* Be careful to focus on serving the needs of the school and the students. If you build friendships based on love, acceptance, and trust, students will want to know *who* you know! Then all you have to do is tell them.

ACTION POINT ☐ Session 20

1. Using the principles from Scripture described in this session, how can you overcome any personal fear of being involved in a Touch Ministry?

2. What steps do you need to take in order to start a Touch Ministry on or around a campus each week?

3. Begin now to compile the following information about your local campus and students.

Number of students in school:

Names of student leaders:

Administrative leaders:

Athletic programs:

Names of coaches:

Extracurricular activities:

Rules for visitors:

Names of school counselors:

Clubs:

Local slang:

4. What are the times and activities where you can best begin a Touch Ministry?

5. Write down the names of three students you know. Jot a little information about each person beside his or her name.

6. To help you work the Touch Ministry into your schedule, make a record of your meetings with students during the rest of the quarter. Include the following information:

Student's Name	Date	Time	Place	What You Talked About

7. Memorize 1 Thessalonians 2:8. Continue your daily times alone with God.

there is one main principle: What needs does the group have—relating to the developmental phase—to help the group progress and grow? To arrive at these needs, a co-working team of counselors spends 30 minutes each night planning the next day, based on their observations and discussions with the group. This allows the counselors to adjust, individualize, and mold programs in response to the group's needs.

The Decentralized Schedule

Although some may consider this heading a contradiction, it is possible to schedule "unscheduled time." Trade Winds Lake Camp, a traditional centralized sleep-away camp located in Windsor, N.Y., adopted into its schedule a block of time from 1:00 to 3:30 every afternoon, in which the responsibility of the day-to-day experience was shifted to the group and the counselors. The counselors were given three categories of

initiatives (team-building, literacy, and recreational), and suggested activities in each of the categories. Counselors chose fewer of the suggested activities, and began to develop their own. Gradually, they were able to respond to the campers' needs, and take more initiative for the experiences of the group. The senior staff reported an immediate effect on group cohesion, team spirit, and overall group performance.

From Outcomes To Experiences

Finally, it's important to mention that a decentralized component can

be introduced into an individual activity. Shifting the focus from specific outcomes to processes is a start. In practical terms, counselors can rethink an activity to turn instructions into questions. For example:

> **We are getting ready to hike three miles.**
> **vs.**
> **How long should our first hike be?**

The question challenges the group to assess what the members already know or need to find out to answer the question. The counselor's job is to guide the conversation and connect the group's choices to available resources and to consider the reality of the group's ability. This also involves allowing the group to fail; if properly mediated, this can be a positive learning experience!

What camps, centralized or decentralized, have in common is they view themselves as educators and role models, adding an essential dimension of a healthy upbringing to countless children each summer. The decentralized approach has the potential to enrich and deepen the campers' experience, and that is—after all—the most important goal.

Note: *Trail Blazer Camps was founded in 1887 by John Ames Mitchell, the original editor of* Life *magazine, who raised $800 to send 266 underprivileged children from New York City to the*  *Life Fresh Air Farm in Branchville, Conn. This past summer was the 125th consecutive year of operation.* ⒸⒷ

Riel Peerbooms is the executive director of Trail Blazer Camps. She can be reached via e-mail at rpeerbooms@trailblazers.org.

> To comment on this article, log on to www.camp-business.com

on the distance and destination of their hike, and the necessary preparations, they have learned important skills and lessons before setting one foot on the trail! Children are given an opportunity not only to experience, but also to take ownership of every aspect of their time at camp. More often than not, the process has allowed all group members—both children and adults— to access and improve skills they did not know they possessed.

Desirable Skills

Operating a fully decentralized program is time-consuming and unpredictable, not to mention the staffing and training requirements it imposes; this is why running a fully decentralized program is so rare in today's summer camps. Yet the decentralized model and many of its elements have much to offer. Here are some ways how decentralized approaches can transform a camper's experience, a counselor's performance, and the short amount of time in camp in a positive way.

Creating The Environment

The most important and immediate improvement in a program is simple: children experience the most learning when you are not trying to teach anything! Much of creating a decentralized program involves preparing the right environment and then having the courage to step aside and let learning occur. This begins with training a counselor to adopt a decentralized mindset, putting him or her in the position of a camper so a counselor can develop as a "mediator" between the camper and the environment, rather than as a teacher structuring that environment for the child. While mock schedules and role-plays are typical elements of most camp-training programs, give staff an actual camper experience for a minimum of two days. This must be experienced as a group, led by seasoned senior counselors. Several broad guidelines (i.e., the types of activities and experiences the group desires) should be the guide. Finally,

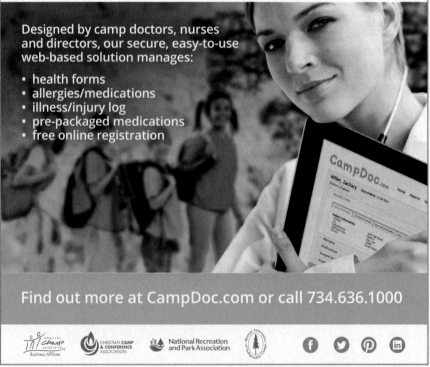

☐ SESSION 21
MATURING STUDENTS IN CHRIST, Part 1

How many people were in your youth group when you were in high school? What percentage of those people do you think are still walking with Christ?

Your estimate may or may not be accurate. But statistics from one of the largest evangelical denominations reveal that only 6 percent of all the students who attend church throughout high school continue to attend regularly when they go to college. Such statistics indicate that "growing up in the church" does not necessarily mean that students will "grow up in Jesus Christ." There must be something more!

Imagine for a moment that you have a Sunday School class or a Bible study where students can learn to study the Bible, memorize Scripture, and witness. As important as those skills are, even a *computer* can be programmed to do them. The process of maturing students involves more than having Bible studies or learning a few skills. It involves making disciples. The process of disciple-making is unique because through it, a *changed life* is created.

Students' lives are transformed through the disciple-making process. As Christians, we are to be "conformed to the likeness of His Son" (Rom. 8:29). In other words, we are to mature in Christ to the point where we begin to take on the likeness of Christ.

Practical Elements of Disciple-Making

Paul understood the uniqueness of disciple-making and knew that discipling others is an essential key to spiritual growth. He gave Timothy some practical insight into how to disciple others: "These things you have heard me say in the presence of many witnesses entrust to reliable men who will also be qualified to teach others" (2 Tim. 2:2). Let's take a closer look at what Paul was saying and identify some underlying elements there.

ELEMENT #1: *RELATIONSHIPS* ("The things *you* have heard *me* say")—Lee was a member of my first discipleship group. I began to reevaluate our group experience when I heard that he had begun taking Jewish confirmation classes. His action told me that our discipleship group hadn't gotten through to him. I knew our material had been good, but we had gone through it in a classroom type setting. I decided to start spending time personally with Lee.

We began meeting together, and over the next couple of months we worked through some of the problems Lee was having in his relationship to God. When we got right down to

the truth, he had never really received Jesus Christ. And it was only within the context of our close relationship that he was able to open up and commit his life to Jesus. Over the next couple of years it took even more time to help Lee grow into a fruitful disciple.

Through that experience, I learned that disciple-making takes place in an atmosphere of love and acceptance. That kind of an atmosphere can only develop through a close personal relationship as we pour our lives into another person.

ELEMENT #2: *REFLECTION* ("Entrust")—When you go to the bank to get something out of your safety-deposit box, you can't do it alone. In addition to your key, you also need the key of the bank official to open the box. The word "entrust" is similar in meaning to taking those two keys and opening the safety-deposit box together.

When Paul tells Timothy to *entrust* what he has heard, his point is to build a trusting relationship in which the riches of the Gospel are transmitted from one person to another. Before Timothy could transmit the Gospel through such a relationship, he had to be committed to reflecting the character of Christ through his life—in attitudes, thoughts, actions, and habits.

Christians are called to be mirrors that "all reflect the Lord's glory" (2 Cor. 3:18). The statement is trite, but true: "Christianity is caught, not taught." If we as leaders are to transmit the Gospel to others, our lives must reflect that Gospel to them.

As people imitate us in the discipling process we:

■ *teach* so that they will gain knowledge.
■ *train* so that they will gain skills.
■ *build* so that they will be strengthened in character.
■ *send* so that they will carry out Christ's vision.

ELEMENT #3: *REALITY* ("In the presence of many witnesses")—This phrase means "in the midst of real-life situations." It has been proven again and again that people respond best to leaders who are *real*. Personally, I find myself sometimes "blowing it" in front of the people I work with. But I've found that what seems to matter most is how I *respond* to blowing it, not the fact that I blew it. The same fact holds true when I get a pat on the back. My responses to success and failure give my co-workers practical examples of Christ working in me. Being real draws us closer together.

Be encouraged by what Paul says about being real: "I came to you in weakness and fear, and with much trembling. My message and my preaching were not with wise and persuasive words, but with a demonstration of the Spirit's power, so that *your faith might not rest on men's wisdom, but on God's power*" (1 Cor. 2:3-5, author's emphasis).

Relax with students and allow them to see both your weaknesses and strengths. They will see Christ living in you through your responses to everyday situations.

ELEMENT #4: *RECRUITING* ("Entrust to reliable men")—

Whom do you disciple? I once worked with a guy who was president of the student body, a big football star, and who dated the head cheerleader. On the outside, he looked like a good candidate for being in a discipleship group. He had expressed a desire to become involved, but I kept putting him off because I sensed that deep down he wasn't really committed. After graduation, he lost the prestige that football and student body leadership had provided. His girlfriend dumped him. He was humbled and began to desire God above all other things. That's when he became ready to be discipled.

When it comes to being a disciple, it is more important what a student is like on the *inside* than what he's like on the *outside*. Potential disciples need to be F-A-T:

Faithful—Desiring what God desires
Available—Taking time to grow
Teachable—Willing to learn

Paul trained F-A-T disciples in the Thessalonian church: "We always thank God for all of you, mentioning you in our prayers. We continually remember before our God and Father your work produced by faith, your labor prompted by love, and your endurance inspired by hope in our Lord Jesus Christ" (1 Thes. 1:2-3).

ELEMENT #5: *REPRODUCTION* ("Qualified to teach others")—Paul had a vision of discipleship that included Timothy and the men he would personally disciple, but also went beyond them to the generations that would follow. Paul writes of *four* levels of discipleship in 2 Timothy 2:2:

Level #1—Paul
Level #2—Timothy
Level #3—Faithful men
Level #4—Others

More people today need to develop Paul's vision. I met and started discipling Bill while he was in college. During that time, Bill became friends with a guy named John. Through their friendship, John became a Christian and was discipled by Bill while they were both on a summer exchange program to the Soviet Union.

One Sunday they attended a Baptist church in Moscow, and after the service a young Russian approached them. He had heard that they were Americans, and because he spoke English, he wanted to talk with them. As they talked, Bill and John discovered that the young Russian man had come to the church because he was searching for meaning and purpose in life.

Bill and John took him to lunch. John spent the rest of the day sharing Christ with the young man, but he was not ready to make a decision to receive Christ. However, the Russian later wrote John and told him that he had become a Christian. Miraculously, he was granted an exit visa and came to the United States for training in Bible and communications. Now he has a Christian radio program that reaches between 10 and 15 million people each day in the Soviet Union.

Discipleship often results in spiritual reproduction far beyond our expectations or imaginations. Spiritual reproduction occurs when:
One maturing believer
Reproduces his faith in other maturing believers
So that they are able to reproduce their faith
In other maturing believers.
This reproduction is the sign of healthy discipleship.

The cost of helping students mature in Christ is high in terms of time, energy, and commitment. The process of disciple-making is much slower than many regular youth programs, but the end result is *changed lives*. Only a few are willing to pay the price of disciple-making, but the ones who pay that price will help change the world. Will you be one of them?

ACTION POINT ☐ Session 21

1. As we begin to think of discipleship in terms of "life change" and not just "knowledge gained," take a few minutes to read through the first two chapters of 1 Thessalonians. Outline the principles that caused Paul to be a "life-changer."

2. As you think about building close personal relationships with students, what are the easiest and hardest things you need to do? Why?

3. Think of one time recently when you felt like you "blew it" in front of the students in your church. What happened? How did you feel?

Now read 2 Corinthians 12:9. What does that verse tell you about always feeling like you have to be a "super" Christian? How can God use times of failure to develop character in your life and in the lives of the students you are working with?

4. What do you need to do to be a better mirror that "reflects the Lord's glory"? (2 Cor. 3:18)

How can you begin to train students who will also reflect the glory of the Lord?

5. Name some F-A-T students in your youth group.

6. Do you really *want* to be a disciple-maker? Why or why not?

7. Memorize 2 Timothy 2:2. Continue your daily times alone with God and readings from Mark.

SESSION 22
MATURING STUDENTS IN CHRIST, Part 2

Think about the people who influenced you while you were growing up. Then single out the one person who had the most influence. Why do you think he or she had such an impact on you?

As leaders, we can be a significant influence on students today. Jesus tells us how we can make a deep and lasting impact on the lives of others. Take a minute to read Matthew 28:18-20. Circle the words "make disciples," because those are the key words in that passage.

The last session contained five elements that should become the basis for our ministry as we disciple others. This session deals with what takes place as students begin to grow toward maturity in Christ through discipleship.

The Authority for Disciple-Making

The beginning point for making disciples is *authority*. Jesus said, "All authority in heaven and on earth has been given to Me" (Matt. 28:18). Having that authority, Jesus had the absolute right to exercize His power using all of the resources of heaven and earth. Disciple-making is characterized by life change because God's supernatural power works in the lives of people. Before we can truly disciple others, we must have authority based on Christ's supernatural power.

Jesus wasn't the sole possessor of God's authority. He told His disciples, "I have given you authority" (Luke 10:19). A judge's authority when he is holding court comes from the power that a higher authority has given him. The same principle is true of Christians. We have Christ's delegated authority because He resides in us and is conforming us to His image.

Because we have Christ's authority, we also have all the resources of heaven and earth available to us. Why is it then, that some people don't experience more power in their lives? The problem stems from a lack of spiritual *maturity*. God doesn't want us to have power that we can't handle. Think in terms of a relationship between a father and his teenage son. The son wants more authority, but sometimes lacks the maturity to respond properly to increased freedom. So the father grants privileges gradually. Similarly, Jesus' authority is unleashed in direct proportion to our levels of maturity to handle it. As Christians mature, more of His power flows through them to others.

The Steps for Disciple-Making

As a youth leader, you have Christ's delegated authority to "go and make disciples." You can impact others' lives through disciple-making in such a way that they will grow to maturity as Christians. In this session, you will look at four stair steps every leader needs to help his student disciple climb. Each step builds on the preceding one(s).

STEP #1 *EVANGELIZE*—Jesus said "Go and make disciples." Implied in His statement is the fact that before a student can *grow* as a disciple, he must first *become* a disciple. So if we are to be disciple-makers, we must first know how to help someone come to know Christ. As leaders, we can follow the example of the early church. Michael Green, a noted author and evangelist from Oxford, says that the early church "gossiped the Gospel." Jesus was *the* topic of conversation because the believers in the early church were convinced that everyone needed to know Jesus Christ.

Jesus modeled a conviction for evangelization throughout His life. He "went through all the towns and villages, teaching in their synagogues, preaching the Good News of the kingdom and healing every disease and sickness. When He saw the crowds, He had compassion on them, because they were harassed and helpless, like sheep without a shepherd. Then He said to His disciples, 'The harvest is plentiful but the workers are few. Ask the Lord of the harvest, therefore, to send out workers into His harvest field' " (Matt. 9:35-38).

Is communicating your faith to others a part of your daily lifestyle? If so, you are already on the road to becoming a disciple-maker. If not, go to your youth minister or pastor and ask him to take you out and show you how to share Christ with others.

STEP #2: *ESTABLISH*—Jesus said, "Make disciples . . . baptizing." The reason Jesus connected "make disciples" with "baptizing" is because baptism identifies people with Jesus. It was His desire that people immediately identify with Him. In order for disciples to become firmly established in their faith, He knew that they must "raise their flag" concerning their new relationship with Him. Baptism was the outward sign for their inner commitment.

After baptism has taken place, growth can take place. Young children pick up habits and attitudes from their parents that are unique to their family. In much the same way, God's children need to be nurtured so they will begin to reflect the character of Christ. (See 1 Thes. 2:7, 11-12.)

This nurturing process was beautifully carried out in Acts 2 as new believers identified with Christ through baptism and then became devoted to the apostles' teaching. All of this commitment was surrounded by an atmosphere of fellowship as they met together daily. Disciples who are never established in the basics of their faith are not likely to continue to grow.

STEP #3 *EQUIP*—Jesus said, "Make disciples . . . teaching." Jesus meant for His followers to move beyond the basics of their faith. Part of the process of development is preparation "for works of service, so that the body of Christ may be built up" (Eph. 4:12). After we firmly establish new believers in their faith, the next step is to help them learn how to equip others.

The disciples became equipped to help others in much the same way as an unskilled carpenter becomes a skilled cabinet-maker—through apprenticeship. Jesus' disciples watched His example, listened to His teaching, and then obeyed His commands. They also received His Spirit. They became equippers.

The early church also understood the importance of equipping. They selected "seven men . . . who are known to be full of the Spirit and wisdom" (Acts 6:3). These men were fully equipped to help others grow. One of the prime marks of a healthy disciple in this stage is that he is ministering to others. The way you teach a student to minister is by letting him see your personal ministry.

STEP #4: *EXTEND*—Jesus said, "Make disciples of all nations." Jesus had this step in mind as the ultimate end to His earthly ministry. He knew He would be leaving all His work in the hands of His disciples. And in order for His disciples to go and make disciples of *all* nations, He knew they must learn to extend their ministry. It's obvious that the disciples learned well from Jesus, because in Acts 1—5, the church *added* to its membership. But from that point on, the church *multiplied.*

As a person moves to the extension level, the relationship between the discipler and the disciple changes. One student described it this way: "When we started out we had a 'father/son' relationship. The leader did the motivating, teaching, and guiding. Then as time went by, he began to give me responsibility for ministering to others. During that time, we moved more to a 'partner' relationship. I remember us often saying that a discipler's responsibility is to work himself out of a job."

When you have moved into a "partner" relationship with your student disciple, you have extended your ministry from one to two. At this level, you are on your way to fulfilling the Great Commission.

As you help others grow to maturity through the disciple-making process, you will experience the ultimate in ministry to students. And you will be able to say with the Apostle Paul:

"For what is our hope, our joy, or the crown in which we will glory in the presence of our Lord Jesus when He comes? Is it not you? Indeed, you are our glory and joy" (1 Thes. 2:19-20).

LEADER
(Feeds feeders)

EXTEND

CO-WORKER
(Feeds others)

EQUIP

DISCIPLE
(Feeds himself)

ESTABLISH

NEW BELIEVER
(Needs to be fed)

EVANGELIZE

NON-CHRISTIAN
(Unfed)

ACTION POINT ☐ Session 22

1. Review STEP #1: *EVANGELIZE*. Beside each of the following characteristics of Jesus' life (taken from Matthew 9:35-38), write out how you think it could relate to you as you work with students:
He related to others.

He was a personal witness.

He had compassion.

He called for laborers.

He asked us to pray.

2. Read Acts 2:41-47. How did new converts in the first-century church begin to grow? Using the following diagram, plug in the verse(s) that applies:

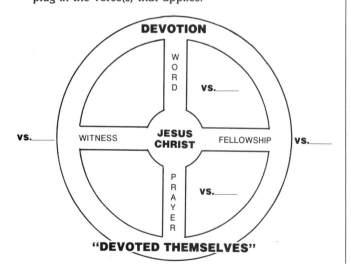

3. Read 1 Thessalonians 1:4-10 and look at the chart below. Describe how Paul established believers in their faith. What is one practical way you can implement each of his principles as you disciple students?

(1) He told them why (v.___) _____

_____

How Paul established them— _____

_____

How you would apply this principle— _____

(2) He showed them how (v.___) _____

How Paul established them— _____

_____

How you would apply this principle— _____

_____

(3) He got them started (v___) _____

_____

How Paul established them— _____

_____

How you would apply this principle— _____

_____

(4) He kept them going (v.___) _____

_____

How Paul established them— _____

_____

How you would apply this principle— _____

_____

(5) He taught them spiritual reproduction (v.___) ___

_____

How Paul established them— _____

_____

How you would apply this principle— _____

_____

4. Read 1 Thessalonians 2:4-12. List five prerequisites to becoming an equipper. Beside each one, explain why you think that would be necessary for equipping someone.

Prerequisites	**Importance of Prerequisites**
(1)	
(2)	
(3)	
(4)	
(5)	

5. What effect do you think this process of discipling (evangelizing, establishing, equipping, and extending) could have on your youth group?

6. In what ways is your church already carrying out the process of discipleship?

7. Memorize Matthew 28:18-20. Continue to fill out a Bible Response Sheet and Prayer Action Sheet every day.

SESSION 23
PRESENTING CHRIST TO STUDENTS

Think about the students you know and list the extracurricular activities that they find fun and exciting. Would you include "going to church" on your list? Unless you were thinking of just Christians, you probably didn't. Going to church just doesn't seem to appeal to secular students—unless someone they respect asks them to go along (or unless your church has a reputation for being "the place to go").

But any church can be "the place to go" if it has the right kind of program. Students need a church meeting they will find interesting and challenging. When Jesus spoke to the crowds, He did things that were exciting. He kept the attention and gained the respect of His audience. Your church can reach students for Jesus Christ in the very same way. If we will make the meetings exciting, Christian students won't be afraid to bring their lost friends.

The Big Event meeting provides an exciting forum to reach unbelieving students with the Gospel of Jesus Christ. The same basic meeting can work for your church too.

What Is The Big Event?

The Big Event is a weekly meeting where the claims of Christ are presented. Jesus used life situations to present Himself to others. He was "living water" to the woman at the well. He was a "fisher of men" to Andrew and Peter (fishermen). He was "the good shepherd," "the great physician," and so forth. And today Jesus needs to be presented to students in a language and atmosphere that they can understand and relate to.

The Big Event is a large group meeting where every student is encouraged to be involved. Wherever Jesus went, crowds were attracted to Him. Mark tells us: "Jesus began to teach by the lake. The crowd that gathered around Him was so large that He got into a boat and sat in it out on the lake, while all the people were along the shore at the water's edge" (Mark 4:1). The Big Event should be a meeting where every student senses the excitement of Jesus Christ.

The Big Event is an evangelistic meeting where Christian students bring lost friends. Jesus called a taxgatherer named Levi to follow Him and become a disciple. Later, Levi had a big, fun event at his house so all of his friends could meet Jesus. "Then Levi held a banquet for Jesus at his house, and a large crowd of tax collectors and others were eating with them" (Luke 5:27-29). In the same way, The Big Event is a fun place for Christian students to bring their lost friends.

Why Is The Big Event Important?

The Big Event provides a meeting structured with just young people in mind. The Big Event should not be planned to meet the needs of the church board, the deacons, or any other age-group (although approval from these other people is important). When young people feel comfortable with the environment, they will be more enthusiastic about inviting their friends to come.

The Big Event makes your "big events" a method of outreach. Time and money previously spent on "fun" outings can now be channeled into evangelism. The idea is to take the time and money spent on other "big" outings and pour it into The Big Event.

The Big Event encourages Christian students. Not only is The Big Event an opportunity for students to have a good time, study the Bible, and talk about Jesus Christ; it is also a time when they see their friends come to know Christ. The Big Event is also a terrific place for young people who are in discipleship groups to minister. Students who are being discipled can bring their friends, witness to them, serve them, counsel them, help them receive Christ, and then follow up on them.

The Big Event visibly brings together all of the other aspects of the Reach Out Strategy. When adult leaders (Leadership Family) are reaching out to students on campus (Touch Ministry), and when students are growing in their faith (Discipleship Ministry), then The Big Event becomes a powerful tool to draw young people to Jesus Christ.

The success of The Big Event is not automatic. The way it is approached will determine its success or failure. A couple of things can kill it from the start.

When adult leaders do not know lost students, The Big Event will become a meeting of Christians only. If you don't lead the way in sharing Jesus Christ with lost students, your student disciples will imitate that attitude and have no desire to reach out to their friends.

If Christian students are not being discipled, they will have no enthusiasm for witnessing. Let's face it, student bodies will never be won without Christian students who can share Christ with their friends. When students are discipled, they will not only have the *ability* to share their faith, but also the enthusiasm that Christ provides. Then they will influence their friends for Jesus Christ.

When Do You Begin The Big Event?

Youth workers can easily fall into the trap of planning only for The Big Event. Even though big events may draw a lot of young people, that approach may fail in the long run because new converts from these meetings are not incorporated into the body of Christ through follow-up and discipleship. So certain building blocks must be set in place before The Big Event begins. If those building blocks are not there, The Big Event will fail.

Building Block #1—*Adult leaders must be committed to the task.*

You need to determine as a group what steps are necessary to start The Big Event program. What will it take to do it? Are you willing to invest the needed money and time? Where does The Big Event fit in? These and other questions have to be answered, and each person in the group should be committed to see the project through.

Building Block #2—*Young people must be involved in discipleship.*

A ministry of discipleship among students gives your young people a vision of what God can do through The Big Event. Their growth in discipleship groups makes them want to see other students know Christ. Active discipleship results in strong student involvement in The Big Event.

Building Block #3—*Young people must be actively sharing their faith.*

Until they develop a desire for evangelism, students will not feel a burden to bring their friends to The Big Event. Your students should be equipped and motivated to share their faith.

Building Block #4—*A Touch Ministry must be in operation.*
How can you expect unbelieving students to attend The Big Event if you have not built relationships with them? The Touch Ministry is the bridge from your church or organization to non-Christian young people. As adults reach out to students on campus, they are opening a channel through which they can draw students to The Big Event.

Building Block #5—*Key church leadership must be supportive.*

Have your adult youth leaders think through the best way to present the need for The Big Event to the church board. You want your pastor and deacons to be behind The Big Event. One suggestion is that you write out your entire strategy (3 to 4 pages) to present to the pastor and other church leaders so they will know where you are headed. Be prayerful. Give them a vision.

And make sure you have a "green light" from the Lord before you begin. He has a way of working out the timing and the smallest details that your best plans can't match. Don't leave Him out of your planning process.

All of these building blocks will help you as an adult leader know the right way to prepare for The Big Event. If it is worth doing, it is worth doing right!

ACTION POINT ☐ Session 23

1. Think back in your own experience as a Christian. What "event" do you remember attending that was of real meaning to you? What made it meaningful?

If not, why? What would need to happen before it could become a viable option?

2. Study 1 Kings 18:20-40. What happened when this real live Big Event took place? What were the elements that made it so exciting?

If yes, what are some of your current activities that may need to be stopped or reevaluated? What barriers would your church face in changing the focus of those activities?

4. Assess the greatest needs of one lost student that you know. How could The Big Event be structured to help him?

3. Realizing that you have limits to your time and priorities, is The Big Event a viable option for your church?

5. Memorize John 7:37-38 and continue your times alone with God.

SESSION 24
BRINGING EVERYTHING TOGETHER

During the past eleven sessions you have seen the different elements that make up a healthy, well-balanced youth ministry: the lordship of Christ, the Leadership Ministry, the Touch Ministry, the Discipleship Ministry, and The Big Event. At this point you should take a few minutes to answer a couple of questions: "What is God's purpose for me as a leader?" and "What is God's purpose for our youth ministry?"

These two questions are closely related. If you don't know God's purpose for your church's youth ministry, it will be hard for you to define your own role as a leader. But the general purpose for any youth ministry is clearly shown in Ephesians 4:11-16. Read the passage and jot down phrases that describe that purpose.

Results of Fruitful Ministry
When you understand the purpose of your ministry and work toward the goal described in Ephesians 4, you can expect certain results: Your group as a whole will be built up and unified, both in faith and in knowledge (Eph. 4:12), and the individual members will "become mature, attaining to the whole measure of the fullness of Christ" (Eph. 4:13).

The purpose of your youth ministry, then, is to provide the type of leaders (Eph. 4:11) who will be able to help your students become mature in Christ (Eph. 4:13).

Signs of Maturity
Students change for the better when they "become mature." They will no longer be "infants, tossed back and forth by the waves, and blown here and there by every wind of teaching" (Eph. 4:14). In other words, when your high school students move on to new environments (college or job), they can be confident that their relationship with Jesus Christ is solid and consistent. They will also begin "speaking the truth in love," and will "in all things grow up into Him who is the Head, that is, Christ" (Eph. 4:15). Students who have assurance that they will continue to grow can help others grow so that the whole body (the church) will be "joined and held together" (Eph. 4:16).

Can you think of any greater joy than seeing your individual students grow to maturity while your youth group grows closer together? But before these results can take place, you must answer the other question posed at the beginning of this session.

"What is God's purpose for me as a leader?" The answer is twofold: (1) to prepare yourself, and (2) to prepare others.

Right now, spend some time in prayer. Thank God for the ways He has already prepared you to help others "become mature." Ask Him to build in you a deep desire to see Ephesians 4:11-16 accomplished in your church's youth ministry. Ask Him to show you specific things you need to commit yourself to do in order to develop maturity and unity in your group.

ACTION POINT ☐ Session 24

1. How well are you prepared to prepare others to become mature? What specific steps can you take to become better prepared?

2. As you analyze your church's youth ministry in light of Ephesians 4:11-16 and the principles of the Reach Out Strategy, how would you evaluate it? When you finish, compare your answers with those you gave for question #2 of the *Action Point* for session 14.

	WHERE WE ARE NOW	**WHERE I'D LIKE US TO BE**
JESUS AS LORD		
LEADERSHIP MINISTRY		
TOUCH MINISTRY		
DISCIPLESHIP MINISTRY		
THE BIG EVENT		

3. Now fill out the Personal Plan of Action below.

PERSONAL PLAN OF ACTION

PLAN OF ACTION	JESUS IS LORD	LEADERSHIP MINISTRY	TOUCH MINISTRY	DISCIPLESHIP MINISTRY	THE BIG EVENT
What goals need to be accomplished?					
What steps must you take to accomplish your goals?					
What is your first step? When will you take it?					
What barriers will you encounter?					
How will you overcome your barriers?					
How can you check your progress?					

4. How would you evaluate the students who are involved in your youth ministry? List appropriate names under each column.

CHRISTIANS	NON-CHRISTIANS	NOT SURE

5. Of the Christian students in your youth ministry, how would you categorize them?

NEW BELIEVER	BEING DISCIPLED	DISCIPLING OTHERS

6. Memorize Ephesians 4:11-13. Continue your daily times with God and readings in Mark.

Important reminder: Make sure you have completed all assignments from Section 2 (daily times alone with God, memory verses, and weekly studies and projects) before moving on to Section 3.

The Leader's Knowledge and Skills for Working with Youth

SESSION 25
DISCOVERING YOUR PURPOSE

[NOTE: For the past 24 sessions, you have been learning what it takes to be a spiritual leader. You have committed yourself to a lifestyle that will continue to strengthen your relationship with the Lord. You have also developed a strategy of ministry that will help you make an impact on the lives of students.

During the next few sessions, the focus will shift to helping you develop the skills necessary to change students' lives. During these final sessions, challenge yourself to pull everything together—your lifestyle, your strategy of ministry, and your skills. As you do, you will discover that you are becoming an effective leader.]

I met Tim (not his real name) in school. He was the stereotype of "tall, dark, and handsome." He was also very intelligent and full of charisma—a natural leader. If that wasn't enough, he also dated a beauty queen. People would see them together and say, "He's so sharp and she's so beautiful; the Lord will *really* use them."

Ten years later, Tim's life was a total washout. He had married the beauty queen. He had gone into the ministry. But somewhere along the way, his relationship with his wife deteriorated and he became involved with another woman. After that, the events in his life started toppling like dominoes—his marriage fell apart, he left his ministry, and moved away.

People often wonder how things like that could ever happen to a guy like Tim. The answer lies below the surface. All of Tim's problems grew out of the fact that his whole life was centered in on his own needs and goals. When his wife stopped meeting his self-centered needs, he turned to someone else.

Another person I remember went through a similar crisis. Craig (also not his real name) had a bout with polio when he was young. He became physically deformed from the waist down, and came out of his crisis filled with insecurity and fear. He wondered what others would think of his physical disability, so he set out to excel in every other area of his life. He built his upper body until it was in great form. He became a "super" Christian. But as a result of *his* determination to become somebody special, Craig developed a harsh and critical attitude toward *others* who didn't measure up to his standards of Christian living.

Craig finally reached a point where he had to stop and do some inner searching. After getting his attitudes squared away with the Lord, he wanted to start meeting with students on

campus, but the thought of going to a high school scared him. What would students think of a cripple like him?

It was at this point of inner crisis that Craig turned to God and began to ask seriously for the first time, "Lord, what is Your purpose for my life?" As God began to reveal His very special purpose, Craig's life began to change. He developed a sense of urgency for reaching students with the Gospel that overcame his self-centered fears of what they would think of him. And God began to transform his harsh criticism of others into love and compassion. The depth of Craig's relationship with God became very evident to those around him. His ministry became recognized by its effective outreach to students—so effective, in fact, that more than 150 students from the campus came to Christ in one month.

Tim and Craig: two men so consumed with their own needs that they couldn't (or didn't want to) see God's purpose for their lives. The result for one was deep personal tragedy. The other sought God's purpose for his life, and the result has been a ministry characterized by fruit and fulfillment.

Jesus spoke very pointedly to this issue when He said:
Do not worry about your life, what you will eat or drink; or about your body, what you will wear. Is not life more important than food, and the body more important than clothes? Look at the birds of the air; they do not sow or reap or store away in barns, and yet your Heavenly Father feeds them. Are you not much more valuable than they? . . . So do not worry, saying, "What shall we eat?" or "What shall we drink?" or "What shall we wear?" For the pagans run after all these things, and your Heavenly Father knows that you need them. But seek first His kingdom and His righteousness, and all these things will be given to you as well (Matt. 6:25-26, 31-33).

God has a special purpose in mind for each of us, but we can miss out on it when we become too consumed with our own interests. We can have all the potential in the world. We can achieve great success with money, power, popularity, family, etc. But potential and personal achievement are not the same as being a success in God's eyes.

It's ridiculous for us *not* to get in on God's purpose for our lives. It's like buying an expensive pen, discovering it doesn't write and saying, "Hey, that's OK. It doesn't really have to write. I just bought it for looks anyway."

Whether it costs us 10¢ or $50, a pen that doesn't write is useless, because the purpose of a pen is to write.

Only after we become aware of God's purpose for us can we begin to see how we can put that purpose into action. Like Craig, our lives can become characterized by fruit and fulfillment after we discover and yield to God's plan for us.

God's Purpose for Our Lives
In Genesis we read that God created many things—animals,

sea, trees, sun, etc. But God created man in His own image. Man has a special purpose. The Prophet Isaiah expressed man's purpose:

> The Spirit of the Sovereign Lord is on me, because the Lord has anointed me to preach good news to the poor. He has sent me to bind up the brokenhearted, to proclaim freedom from the captives and release for the prisoners, to proclaim the year of the Lord's favor and the day of vengeance of our God, to comfort all who mourn, and provide for those who grieve in Zion—to bestow on them a crown of beauty instead of ashes, the oil of gladness instead of mourning, and a garment of praise instead of a spirit of despair. They will be called oaks of righteousness, a planting of the Lord for the display of His splendor (Isa. 61:1-3).

God has redeemed us so we may "display His splendor."

Jesus acknowledged God's purpose for man when He prayed: "I in them and You in Me. May they be brought to complete unity to let the world know that You sent Me" (John 17:23).

Paul sheds some more light on God's purpose for man when he says, "We, who with unveiled faces all reflect the Lord's glory" (2 Cor. 3:18). In revelation, John describes how we will glorify God for all eternity:

> Then I looked and heard the voice of many angels, numbering thousands upon thousands, and ten thousand times ten thousand. They encircled the throne and the living creatures and the elders. In a loud voice they sang: "Worthy is the Lamb, who was slain, to receive power and wealth and wisdom and strength and honor and glory and praise!" Then I heard every creature in heaven and on earth and under the earth and on the sea, and all that is in them, singing: "To Him who sits on the throne and to the Lamb be praise and honor and glory and power, for ever and ever!" (Rev. 5:11-13)

Our purpose as Christians is to glorify God—to reflect His image to the world. That's why He created us; that's why He has redeemed us. But how do we go about "reflecting the Lord's glory?" Paul goes on to tell us that we "are being transformed into His likeness with ever-increasing glory, which comes from the Lord, who is the Spirit" (2 Cor. 3:18). He also said: "For those God foreknew He also predestined to be conformed to the likeness of His Son" (Rom. 8:29).

Summary

Paul summarizes our purpose in very practical terms when he says, "So whether you eat or drink or whatever you do, do it all for the glory of God" (1 Cor. 10:31).

Our purpose in life is to glorify God. We glorify Him by reflecting His image to the world. We reflect His image to the world by becoming conformed to His Son.

During the next few sessions, we will get practical about our purpose in life and see how it affects our relationship with God and our relationships with others.

ACTION POINT ☐ Session 25

1. Summarize in one or two sentences God's purpose for your life.

2. Read Ephesians 1:3-14 and reflect on who you are in Christ. Write a paragraph on who you are in relationship to Him.

3. Read Philippians 1:6. Think about two specific illustrations from your life describing how God has already begun to accomplish His purpose by doing "a good work in you."

4. Now read Jeremiah 29:11-13. God has a great future in store for you. If you could cast aside all restraint and think about your biggest dream for how God might glorify Himself through you, what would your dream be?

Dwell on that dream through the next four sessions and think of ways for that dream to become a reality.

5. Memorize 1 Corinthians 10:31 and continue your daily times alone with God.

SESSION 26
DEFINING YOUR PERSONAL GOALS

About a year and a half after I became a Christian, I was sitting in my room at Davidson College. The thought came to me, *Barry, maybe you shouldn't be playing basketball.* My next thought went something like, *St. Clair, that's about the dumbest idea you've ever had.*

I had been playing basketball from the time I was in first grade. Since fourth grade I'd been playing on organized teams. In the winter I would sweep the snow off the outside court and play basketball with my gloves on. During the summer before my senior year in high school, I practiced eight hours ever day so I could play up to my maximum potential the next season.

Everything in my life revolved around "the game." I wanted nothing more than to play college basketball and, perhaps, to make the all-conference team. Quitting was out of the question, so I pushed the thought out of my mind.

But the thought kept coming back—*Maybe you shouldn't be playing basketball.* One day I was reading the Bible and my eyes froze on Matthew 6:33: "But seek first His kingdom and His righteousness, and all these things will be given to you as well."

"Seek first what God wants," the verse seemed to say to me. And I had to admit to myself, *Barry, you've been a Christian for a year and a half, but you've never given basketball to the Lord. Basketball is your goal, not God's.*

God seemed to be asking, "Are you more serious about pursuing My goals or yours?" Giving up basketball while I was in college was my first difficult step toward pursuing God's goals instead of mine. And as I began to grow in my understanding of God's goals for me, I found a great theme in the New Testament. When Jesus was asked to state the greatest commandment, He answered: " 'Love the Lord your God with all your heart and with all your soul and with all your mind, [and with all your strength.]' This is the first and greatest commandment. And the second is like it: 'Love your neighbor as yourself' " (Matt. 22:37-39 [Luke 10:27]).

I saw that God's purpose of glorifying Himself through me would be accomplished when I made it my goal to fulfill this Great Commandment by loving Him. Jesus tells us clearly how that happens. He says to love Him:

- With all your heart (Spiritually)
- With all your soul (Socially)
- With all your mind (Mentally)
- With all your strength (Physically)

These four areas encompass God's objectives for each of us when it comes to our personal lives.

Loving God Spiritually

Learning to love God wholeheartedly is a continual spiritual discipline. Obedience is hard, but so is anything of value. As the sign in the locker room reads, "No pain, no gain." Spiritual disciplines are not legalistic rules to keep, but doorways to freedom. They open the door into the presence of God. They put us in the place where God can change us to become the people He purposed us to be.

The story is told of a great sculptor who said to one of his apprentices, "You see that block of marble over there? That block of marble is really a horse. My job is to chip away everything that doesn't look like a horse." As we know and love God more and more, our obedience allows Him to chip away everything that keeps us from becoming more like Him.

Loving God Socially

As a member of a fraternity in college, I had to face some tough decisions in my social life. Many of the guys in the fraternity were into drinking and partying. The decision boiled down to deciding whether my fraternity brothers' friendships were important enough to make me compromise what I knew God wanted me to do. I decided against the compromise. As a result, God showed me that He would be my friend and bring other friends into my life who would support and encourage me as a Christian. After making that decision, I began to look to God to show me how to love Him in all of my social life.

Out of my fraternity experience came my objective to cultivate the ability to be a true friend and to build true friendships—not on the basis of what people could do to help me, but what I could do to care for them. God will work in your personality to develop friendships when your objective is to love Him with all of your soul.

Loving God Mentally

Soon after I got to college, I discovered that I was no longer the terrific success I had been in high school. I had set some academic goals—deciding that I was going to be at least a B student. My first test was in history, my intended major. I studied like crazy. But when the test results came back, I found out I had made a 74—a D. I had never made a D in my life.

Being the self-sufficient person that I was, I decided I would just have to study harder. I spent as much time as I possibly could preparing for the next test. I didn't get a 74 on that one; I got a 47! My academic goals were slipping down the tube fast. It was as if all the props I had depended on were being knocked out from under me. It didn't help that one of my roommates was a Fulbright Scholar and one of my fraternity brothers was a Rhodes Scholar.

My shaky start in college made me feel very inferior mentally. But some time later, God began to make real to me the truth of Romans 12:2: "Do not conform any longer to the pattern of this world, but be transformed by the renewing of your mind." I discovered that when I came to know Jesus Christ, I was given the mind of Christ (Phil. 2:5). And I finally began to see that God had created my mind the way He wanted it to be in order to use me in the best way possible.

I've learned that my personal objective of "loving God with all my mind" is to learn to think God's thoughts, which are so much higher than my thoughts (Isa. 55:8-9). Loving God mentally involves consistently studying God's Word and helping people understand what He has taught me.

Loving God Physically

Because I've always been into sports, I've never really had any problems keeping myself in shape. But after I graduated from college, I began to realize that I had always taken such good care of myself for the wrong reason—to be at my best for athletics. God began to show me that His purpose for me keeping physically fit was totally different. God wanted me to care for my body because it is His temple (1 Cor. 6:19).

Physical discipline is important. Through exercise, diet, and rest, we can keep our bodies in top shape so that God gets the maximum performance out of them—for His glory.

Defining your goals and objectives for each of these areas isn't something meant to put you on a guilt trip. It's a method of determining what God wants you to do so that you can walk through the doorway of loving Him.

ACTION POINT ☐ Session 26

1. Meditate on Jeremiah 29:11-13. Think about the dream you described in the last session (*Action Point* Question #4). Consider how this session on loving God with all your heart, soul, mind, and strength fits into your dream of glorifying God to the maximum. Write your thoughts here.

2. Are you sometimes reluctant to consider "lifetime goals"? You shouldn't be. They can help you take your dream and see it become reality. This exercise will help you break down your dream into measurable, bite-sized chunks (objectives). On the chart that follows, consider the spiritual, social, mental, and physical areas of your life, and write down at least one objective for each area. Take time to pray and reflect as you go. Make certain that what you write is really what you want to do.

PERSONAL OBJECTIVES	
1. Spiritual	
2. Social	
3. Mental	
4. Physical	

3. Memorize Matthew 22:36-38. Continue your daily Bible study from the Book of Mark.

SESSION 27
REFINING YOUR RELATIONSHIPS

I had a lot of "friends" in high school, but often I was selfish and used them to accomplish *my* goals. I didn't really love them. After I met Jesus Christ, and began to apply His Great Commandment (to love God with my heart, soul, strength, and mind), my attitudes toward others began to change. Slowly I began to see the rest of Jesus' Great Commandment take root as I learned to love my neighbor as myself (Matt. 22:39)—particularly where my parents, my sister, and my friends were concerned.

This second part of the Great Commandment is an essential part of glorifying God. Jesus said that our love for each other is the evidence that we belong to Him (John 13:34-35). The kind of love He describes is God-centered love. Paul explains how we should practice God's love toward each other: "Do nothing out of selfish ambition or vain conceit, but in humility consider others better than yourselves. Each of you should not look only to your own interests, but also to the interests of others" (Phil. 2:3-4).

Before you go on, stop right now and pray to receive the humility to consider other people and their interests as more important than your own. God is the only One who can provide that kind of love toward others.

Loving My Neighbor: Family
Loving others begins with our families. How can we express God's love to them? If you are a husband, you have the privilege of loving your wife as Christ loved the church—sacrificially (Eph. 5:24). If you are a parent, you can express your love to your children by bringing them up in the discipline and instruction of the Lord (Eph. 6:4). If you are a wife, you can demonstrate your love for your husband by respecting and honoring him (Eph. 5:23-24). And if you are a son or daughter, you can show your love to your parents by obeying them (Eph. 6:1-3).

If you are single, then your parents, brothers, and sisters are the central focus of your love. If you are married, your wife or husband is the center of your thoughts. If you have children, your horizons will broaden to include them. (If you don't have a family, adopt one! Many families in your church have love to spare and need your love in return.)

Be specific as you begin to show love in practical ways within your family roles. For example, since I am a husband and father, I am a prophet for my family. As a prophet, I am to teach my family God's Word. So one of my objectives is, "Plan and carry out an enjoyable 15-minute devotional time Monday through Friday for my family." Setting specific objectives helps me know exactly what to do.

The following diagrams will help you visualize your objectives in loving your family:

SON OR DAUGHTER	
SEEKER—Seek after God and be an example to your family.	SUPPLICATOR—Pray for your family.
SENSITIZER—Communicate in such a way that you help the others in your family be sensitive to each other.	SERVANT—Look for ways to minister to the other members of your family.

HUSBAND, FATHER, SINGLE PARENT	
PROPHET—Teach God's Word to your family and live it out before them.	PRIEST—Pray for your family. Set aside times for the family to pray together.
PROVIDER—Make wise financial decisions.	PAL—Be your family's best friend.

WIFE, MOTHER	
MATE—Support your husband's goals for his life as his "helper."	MOTHER—Train your children to love God.
MOTIVATOR—Create and direct the activities of your family.	MINISTER—Be a Proverbs 31 type of woman who meets the needs of her family.

Loving My Neighbor: Friends
But we have other relationships outside of our families. These "significant others" are included in Jesus' Great Commandment to love our neighbors as ourselves.

One great example of true friendship is the story of David and Jonathan (1 Sam. 18:1-4). From their friendship, we can discover four levels of deepening relationships:

(1) *Attraction*—The initial stage of getting to know each other. (v. 1)
(2) *Affection*—The level of sharing common experiences built around common goals. (v. 1)
(3) *Accountability*—The degree of concern that holds the other person responsible for developing the character of Christ in his or her life. (v. 3)
(4) *Agape*—The highest level of love in which one friend is willing to die for the other. (v. 4)

Meaningful friendships can be developed at any of these four levels. And as two people express love toward one another, their relationship will move from one level to the next.

Do you have three friends with whom you can share *every* feeling and circumstance of your life? As you consider your friendships, ask yourself the following questions:

(1) Where is the best place for me to meet new people?

(2) Am I willing to give of myself to deepen my friendships?

(3) Do I share common goals with my current friends?

(4) Am I committed to any of my friends enough to give my life for them?

Don't underestimate the importance of friendship. Remember that each person you meet is a divine appointment that has friendship potential. As you pursue the goals you set for your family and friends, you will enjoy a sense of fulfillment that can only be superseded by the love you have for God Himself.

ACTION POINT ☐ Session 27

1. Read Galatians 5:13-14. These verses will help clarify how your family and friends fit into your goal of glorifying God to the maximum. Record your thoughts about how these verses tie into your life goal.

2. Examine your family relationships. Select the family relationship described in this session that best describes you (daughter, for example), record your four roles below, and write an objective that will help you perform each new role more effectively.

FAMILY OBJECTIVES	
Role	Objective
1.	
2.	
3.	
4.	

3. Now think about your friendships. For each of the following levels of friendship, think of one person whom you would include in that level. Then write an objective for each level that will help you develop a stronger relationship with that friend.

FRIENDSHIP OBJECTIVES		
Level	Name	Objective
1. Attraction		
2. Affection		
3. Accountability		
4. Agape		

Remember: You are writing "lifetime objectives," so don't be overwhelmed by them. Later on, you will see how these lifetime objectives can be broken down into one-year objectives that you will be able to achieve.

4. Memorize John 15:13 and keep up your times alone with God.

SESSION 28
DESIGNING YOUR MINISTRY

Lee is a businessman. His wife, Sue, is a homemaker and mother of two. Both of them enjoy what they are doing and feel that God has led them to their respective responsibilities. And both of them love students. Lee gets off from work every afternoon and heads over to the high school to watch and encourage the players and cheerleaders of whatever team happens to be practicing. Sue helps plan the youth activities for their church. Together they sponsor a Leadership Family and work with students in discipleship groups.

Work and church are two areas that often seem miles apart. But Lee and Sue have made them come together effectively. How have they done it? More importantly, how can *you* do it?

Lee and Sue are normal people, but they have determined to do whatever they can to fulfill Jesus' Great Commission: "Go and make disciples of all nations, baptizing them in the name of the Father and of the Son and of the Holy Spirit, and teaching them to obey everything I have commanded you. And surely I will be with you always, to the very end of the age" (Matt. 28:19-20). The Great Commission is the second goal that God has for our lives. (The first goal is the Great Commandment discussed in sessions 26 and 27).

Jesus expresses His second goal for us in another way: "You will receive power when the Holy Spirit comes on you; and you will be My witnesses in Jerusalem, and in all Judea and Samaria, and to the ends of the earth" (Acts 1:8). "Jerusalem" for *us* is the place we spend most of our time. If you are like most people, your two major time commitments outside of your home are your job and your church. These are the places where we need to first put the Great Commission into action.

God's desire is that we will glorify Him by responding to the Great Commission at our jobs and in our church ministries. We can fulfill His desire for us in two ways. First, we can demonstrate *excellence* in our jobs and church ministries. The Bible challenges us to excellence: "Whatever you do, work at it with all your heart, as working for the Lord, not for men, since you know that you will receive an inheritance from the Lord as a reward. It is the Lord Christ you are serving" (Col. 3:23-24). The second thing we can do is to use our jobs and church ministries as opportunities to *influence* others for Jesus Christ. We should be God's representatives wherever we are. "We are therefore Christ's ambassadors, as though God were making His appeal through us. We implore you on Christ's behalf: Be reconciled to God" (2 Cor. 5:20). Consider the following suggestions for setting job and church ministry objectives under the goals of the Great Commission.

Job Objectives

1. *Supplication*—We need to pray about our jobs—to perform with excellence, to minister to the people we work with, and to be a positive influence on the events, activities, and projects which are coming up in the office.

2. *Study*—We need to set aside time to think through, read about, and plan out goals in our jobs so we can become experts at what we do.

3. *Supervising*—We are to oversee people by encouraging them in ways that will make them successful. We should never see a supervisory role in terms of superiority or a cold, heartless dedication to duty, but rather a compassionate concern for the people under us.

4. *Shepherding*—We show our spiritual concern for others by shepherding. When a person who works for us is lost, shepherding means taking the initiative to share the Gospel of Jesus Christ with him. If the people who work for us are Christians, we shepherd them by challenging them to grow spiritually. This could be as simple as a word of encouragement or as involved as starting a weekly Bible study.

An eight-hour work day becomes exciting when you see your job as a ministry.

Church Ministry Objectives

1. *Supplication*—Pray by name for the young people you are responsible for. Also remember your youth workers and youth events in prayers. Write specific requests in your Time Alone with God notebook and then pray for certain ones on different days of the week.

2. *Study*—Prepare for your specific responsibilities in youth ministry by setting aside time to think them through, plan them out, and set goals that will enable you to accomplish your commitments with excellence.

3. *Supervising*—Sometimes your responsibilities will include overseeing a group of young people or adults. Set goals for those responsibilities whether you are asked to supervise the cooking at a retreat or to lead a discipleship family.

4. *Shepherding*—Again, this is the area where you show spiritual concern for others. Whether offering a word of encouragement, enlisting students for a Bible study group, or meeting with people one-to-one, you always need to ask yourself, *Where is that person spiritually? How can I help that person take the next step?*

Following this plan of supplication, study, supervising, and shepherding, you will thoroughly cover every area of ministry—both at your job and in your church. As you minister to others, you will reach *your* maximum potential as you help others reach *their* maximum potential.

Let the truth of Jesus' Great Commission capture you. Pair it with the Great Commandment and make them part of God's goal that you will "reflect His image" to the people around you.

ACTION POINT ☐ Session 28

1. Read Colossians 3:23. This verse will clarify how your job and church ministry fit into your dream of glorifying God to the maximum. Express your thoughts concerning how the two fit together.

2. Focus on your lifetime goals for your job. Write one objective for each of the suggested roles described in this session.

JOB OBJECTIVES	
	Objective
1. Supplication	
2. Study	
3. Supervising	
4. Shepherding	

3. Now do the same thing for your church ministry objectives.

CHURCH MINISTRY OBJECTIVES	
	Objective
1. Supplication	
2. Study	
3. Supervising	
4. Shepherding	

4. Review your responses to the Action Points for Sessions 26, 27, and 28. Transfer your objectives to the My Lifetime Goals sheet on the next page. When you finish, photocopy the sheet and keep the copy in a place where you can review your goals often.

5. Memorize Acts 1:8. Remember to review previous memory verses on a regular basis and continue your daily prayer and Bible study.

MY LIFETIME GOALS
Purpose: To glorify God (1 Corinthians 10:31)

Goal #1: Fulfill the Great Commandment (Matthew 22:36-38)

PERSONAL OBJECTIVES

1. Spiritual—
2. Social—
3. Mental—
4. Physical—

FAMILY OBJECTIVES (Fill in the four role responsibilities that apply to you)

1.
2.
3.
4.

FRIENDSHIP OBJECTIVES

1. Attraction—
2. Affection—
3. Accountability—
4. Agape—

Goal #2: Fulfill the Great Commission (Matthew 28:18-20)

JOB OBJECTIVES

1. Supplication—
2. Study—
3. Supervising—
4. Shepherding—

CHURCH MINISTRY OBJECTIVES

1. Supplication—
2. Study—
3. Supervising—
4. Shepherding—

SESSION 29
USING TIME WISELY

Do you ever feel like a frustrated juggler as you try to balance your personal life, family, friends, job, and church activities? One of the biggest struggles in life is staying balanced, but it is not an impossible goal. Jesus lived a balanced life. He grew "in wisdom and stature, and in favor with God and men" (Luke 2:52).

God's desire for us is balanced living. A balanced life begins with knowing where you want to go, what your plan is to get there, and how to carry your plan through. But even now, maybe you are wondering how you will handle all of the objectives you've outlined on your Lifetime Goals sheet.

Achieving a balanced lifestyle is a lot like focusing a single lens reflex camera. When you look into the viewfinder, if the picture is out of focus, you will see two distinct and separate images. In order to focus the picture, you keep turning the dial until the two images become one sharp image. During the past four sessions you have been focusing the lens of what your life must be like if you are to achieve your dream of glorifying God to the maximum. In this session we want to start changing the focus of your present lifestyle to become that of your dreams until they eventually become one distinct picture—a picture that "reflects the image of God in this world."

Using Time Wisely

Paul tells us: "Be very careful, then, how you live—not as unwise but as wise, making the most of every opportunity, because the days are evil" (Eph. 5:15-16). When he says, "Be very careful," he means to measure exactly and accurately the way we conduct ourselves. Then he says that the way we can do that is by "making the most of every opportunity." So we need to make wise and sacred use of our time.

Our use of time is far more important than our use of money. We can save money and invest it, gain interest and reinvest it. But *time can never be saved. It can only be spent.*

God has called each one of us to be good stewards of our time. When we begin to spend our time wisely, we will notice several positive advantages:

(1) Our work gets done more quickly and we find time for other things.

(2) We have a sense of accomplishment, rather then feeling guilty or perplexed about where our time went.

(3) We are relieved of the frustration of, "What do I do next?"

(4) Decisions can be made in peaceful moments instead of crisis situations.

(5) We dictate the use of our energy rather than having others plan our time for us.

(6) We maintain a plan to stay on track.

(7) Decisions and plans can be made as we see all of the variables clearly in front of us.

(8) We are protected from burnout because we can see how we are using our time rather than drifting from moment to moment, activity to activity.

The proper use of your time must be developed. You will not instantly "know" how to manage your time, but as you "bump into the walls," you will get a feel for any changes you need to make. And as you learn to use the right tools, you will discover more and more freedom. The tools that will help you use time wisely are one-year objectives, a set of priorities, and your schedule.

One-year Goals—In the last session, you should have completed a sheet of "My Lifetime Goals." Now you need to take those lifetime objectives and break them down into one-year objectives. As you look at each lifetime objective, ask the simple question: "What does God want me to do *this* year?" As you record each one-year objective, make sure it is measurable and set a deadline date for seeing that it gets done.

Priorities—Once those one-year goals are completed, you need to prioritize them. Determine which goals are most important by assigning each one either an "A" (absolutely must be done), "B" (very important), or "C" (important, but can wait until later).

Schedule—Most people do not like to follow a schedule, especially those who need it the most. But a schedule demands that you use your time more wisely. It is like a map of your goals, objectives, and priorities which leads to your destination— glorifying God. These hints will help you use your schedule most effectively:

(1) Write out your *actual* schedule (not how you wish it would be) in 30-minute segments.

(2) List your present commitments, appointments, and the time you spend weekly for each one.

(3) Compare your goals and objectives with your present commitments. What conflicts do you discover?

(4) Write out a revised weekly schedule—one in which you have resolved any conflicts between your present commitments and your goals and objectives. Try it out for a week. Rearrange it where necessary. Then plan every week around this "ideal schedule."

(5) Keep a daily schedule and calendar. (I personally recommend that you write Daytimers, Inc., Allentown, PA 18001 for a catalogue.) A daily schedule helps you meet your objectives on a short-term basis.

(6) Communicate your schedule to your family. Talk it through with them so that they share your goals, priorities, and time commitments.

(7) Make a "To Do" list. Each day write down your six most significant things to do that day in order of priority.

(8) Use your waiting time wisely. Always keep one or two short projects with you (jotting a note, making a quick call, reviewing memory verses, reading a few pages of a book, etc.).

(9) Watch out for these time wasters:

Disorganization	Television
Lack of delegation	Lack of planning
Unnecessary interruptions	Attending unnecessary meetings
Procrastination	Tiredness
Reading junk mail	Lack of promptness

Remember—Time is life! You are spending time whether you are doing anything worthwhile or not. Use your time to accomplish what God wants for your life!

ACTION POINT ☐ Session 29

1. What does God's Word challenge us to do about the use of our time?
   Psalm 90:1-2, 12

   Ephesians 5:15-16

   Colossians 4:5-6

2. Review your Lifetime Goals from last session, then fill out the following One-Year Goals Sheet. Adapt each of your lifetime objectives into a measurable, short-term objective, and set a deadline for each one. (Example: If your lifetime "Shepherding" goal under Church Objectives is "To make evangelism a priority in my ministry," your one-year goal for the same section might be "To share Christ in personal evangelism with at least one person each week" [2-hour commitment].) Writing these one-year objectives will take time and thought.

   When you finish, prioritize your objectives by rating each one with an "A" (Absolutely must be done), a "B" (Very important), or a "C" (Important, but can wait until later).

3. Keep a Daily Time Log this week. It will help you see how you are actually spending your time. Put a check (✔) beside the activities that are part of your one-year goals, and use the same "A," "B," and "C" priority system to evaluate your current activities.

4. Memorize Ephesians 5:15-16. Continue your daily times alone with God.

MY ONE-YEAR GOALS
Purpose: To glorify God (1 Corinthians 10:31)

Goal #1: Fulfill the Great Commandment (Matthew 22:36-38)	DUE DATE	TIME ESTIMATE
PERSONAL OBJECTIVES 1. Spiritual— 2. Social— 3. Mental— 4. Physical— FAMILY OBJECTIVES (Fill in the four role responsibilities that apply to you.) 1. 2. 3. 4. FRIENDSHIP OBJECTIVES 1. Attraction— 2. Affection— 3. Accountability— 4. Agape—		

Goal #2: Fulfill the Great Commission (Matthew 28:18-20)	DUE DATE	TIME ESTIMATE
JOB OBJECTIVES 1. Supplication— 2. Study— 3. Supervising— 4. Shepherding— CHURCH MINISTRY OBJECTIVES 1. Supplication— 2. Study— 3. Supervising— 4. Shepherding—		

DAILY TIME LOG

TIME	SUNDAY ACTIVITY	ONE-YEAR GOAL?	PRIORITY	MONDAY ACTIVITY	ONE-YEAR GOAL?	PRIORITY	TUESDAY ACTIVITY	ONE-YEAR GOAL?	PRIORITY	WEDNESDAY ACTIVITY	ONE-YEAR GOAL?	PRIORITY	THURSDAY ACTIVITY	ONE-YEAR GOAL?	PRIORITY	FRIDAY ACTIVITY	ONE-YEAR GOAL?	PRIORITY	SATURDAY ACTIVITY	ONE-YEAR GOAL?	PRIORITY
6:00																					
6:30																					
7:00																					
7:30																					
8:00																					
8:30																					
9:00																					
9:30																					
10:00																					
10:30																					
11:00																					
11:30																					
NOON																					
12:30																					
1:00																					
1:30																					
2:00																					
2:30																					
3:00																					
3:30																					
4:00																					
4:30																					
5:00																					
5:30																					
6:00																					
6:30																					
7:00																					
7:30																					
8:00																					
8:30																					
9:00																					
9:30																					
10:00																					
10:30																					
11:00																					
11:30																					

SESSION 30
GETTING ON SCHEDULE (Group Project)

[This session is designed as a group project, but the extra time spent laying out and refining your schedule won't be wasted on an individual level. If you are not part of a group yet and need a little more time to nail down the priorities in your personal life and in your ministry, proceed with this session before moving on to Session 31. Adapt instructions to the group to meet your specific needs.]

The purpose of this session is to build on last session's *Action Point* activities and establish workable schedules for yourself and your youth ministry. Complete your personal schedule on your own and then work with the group to design your youth ministry schedule.

Developing Your Personal Schedule

Step #1—Take about 15 minutes to review your prioritized One-Year Goals (from last session's *Action Point*) and compare them with the Daily Time Log you kept during the past week. Spend a few minutes in prayer asking God for wisdom as you begin to work through your schedule.

Step #2—Prioritize the activities on your Daily Time Log using the "A," "B," and "C" ratings if you haven't yet done so.

Step #3—Create an Ideal Weekly Schedule which includes both your One-Year Goals and the "A" priorities from your Daily Time Log. Then add your "B" priorities and (if you still have time in your schedule) "C" priorities. If you aren't able to include all of your "B" and "C" priorities, keep in mind that by leaving them out you are actually taking the necessary steps to accomplish your top goals and objectives.

Step #4—Evaluate the relationship between your youth ministry and your personal schedule/priorities. Have you allowed enough time for effective youth ministry? Too much? Be realistic.

Step #5—Use your Ideal Weekly Schedule to plan your schedule for the next week. After you write out a schedule for the coming week, try to stick to it as closely as possible.

Step #6—Meet with your group leader and have him evaluate your proposed schedule for this week. Ask for his objective opinion to determine whether you are scheduling too much or too little time for activities you aren't sure about.

Remember:
- It often takes twice as long to do something as you would normally think.
- Build flexibility into your schedule by planning for interruptions.
- Don't feel guilty if you don't reach all your goals on the first try. Just keep refining your schedule.

Developing a Youth Ministry Schedule

Step #1—As a group, evaluate your group leader's ministry goals and priorities.

Step #2—Your group leader should provide a tentative youth ministry schedule. Revise what he has done to set up two workable youth ministry schedules—one for the year and another to use on a week-by-week basis.

Step #3—Determine how your goals fit into the youth ministry goals and how your schedule overlaps with the youth ministry schedule. Discuss your findings with the group.

NOTES:

SESSION 31
DISCOVERING YOUR SPIRITUAL GIFTS

What is your spiritual gift? Before you think of an *answer* to the question, what are your *reactions* to hearing the question?

Perhaps you had one of these reactions:

(1) "I'm not going to answer this. Discussions of spiritual gifts can lead to bizarre topics like handling snakes."

(2) "I play the piano on Sunday mornings."

(3) "I don't have the foggiest idea."

Perhaps one of the most serious deficiencies in the church today is the lack of knowledge and understanding concerning spiritual gifts. If you are unaware of your specific spiritual gift(s), you are not alone. But it is vitally important that you discover your gift(s) so you will be able to minister to students at the point of your greatest strengths.

You may feel uncomfortable discussing spiritual gifts because of your background, an unclear understanding of what they are, or other reasons. But spiritual gifts are the muscle of ministry for the church. So try to set aside any hesitation you may have for a few minutes and be willing to learn.

Why Have Spiritual Gifts?

Spiritual gifts are part of God's resources to accomplish His ministry here on earth. They are not to be confused with human abilities or talents. Some people have great talents and abilities which tend to focus on the individual who possesses such talents. But spiritual gifts are given to *all* Christians when they make their life commitments to Christ. (See Rom. 12:5-8 and 1 Cor. 12:7.) Spiritual gifts should not draw attention to one's self, but should be used for service to others. *They are a supernatural endowment by God to a believer for accomplishing God's work.*

What Are the Spiritual Gifts?

Paul helps us distinguish between three categories of spiritual gifts in 1 Corinthians 12:4-6: "There are *different kinds of gifts,* but the same Spirit. There are *different kinds of service,* but the same Lord. There are *different kinds of working,* but the same God works all of them in all men" (author emphasis).

Paul mentions three groupings of gifts, each of which serves a different purpose. "Different kinds of gifts" (*grace gifts*) give us motivation for ministry. They serve as the basic inner drive which God places in each Christian to build His church. A list of grace gifts is found in Romans 12:4-8.

"Different kinds of service" (*service gifts*) are the gifts we receive to empower our ministry to others within the church. Lists of these gifts can be found in Ephesians 4:11 and 1 Corinthians 12:27-31.

"Different kinds of working" (*working gifts*) are the manifestations of these gifts as a result of the Holy Spirit working through our lives. A list of working gifts are found in 1 Corinthians 12:7-11.

As we think about our spiritual gifts, we should begin with our motivational gift (*grace gift*), because that gift motivates us to minister in a certain way. It also provides the greatest amount of joy when we use it. I think Scripture supports the view that each Christian receives only one motivational (*grace*) gift (1 Cor. 7:7; 1 Tim. 4:14-15; 2 Tim. 1:6; 1 Peter 4:10). If some people received two or more gifts from God while others received only one, the tendency of the first group would be to become spiritually proud and boastful. But if everyone receives only one basic gift, all people are equally needed in the body of Christ to accomplish the ministry in His church. When no one is more important than another, it is easier to depend on each other.

However, from each person's *grace gift* can come a variety of different *service gifts.* And then when someone exercises his service gift through his ministry, any number of *working gifts* may be manifested. So let's look closer at these grace gifts that motivate our ministries.

Grace Gifts

At least seven gifts fall into the category of grace gifts (based on Rom. 12:4-8):

(1) Prophecy—This gift declares truth or reveals ungodly motives and attitudes by presenting God's truth. (See 1 Cor. 14:6-12.)

(2) Serving—This gift demonstrates love by meeting practical needs. (See Gal. 5:13.)

(3) Teaching—This gift clarifies truth or validates truth that has been presented. (See Col. 3:16.)

(4) Encouraging—This gift stimulates the faith of others. (See Heb. 3:13.)

(5) Giving—This gift entrusts resources to others for the furtherance of ministry. (See 2 Cor. 9:6-8.)

(6) Leadership—This gift coordinates the activities of others for the achievement of common goals. (See Heb. 13:17.)

(7) Mercy—This gift identifies with and comforts those who are in distress. (See Luke 6:36.)

God wants you to discover your spiritual gift and express it! But how can you know which gift God has given you?

Practical Guidelines for Discovering Your Spiritual Gift

Six factors play a vital role in discovering your spiritual gift(s):

(1) *Faith.* You have to believe through faith that God has gifted you based on what He has said. (See John 15:16.) Once you are fairly sure what your gift is, act on your faith by taking advantage of opportunities to exercise that gift.

(2) *Prayer.* Ask God for understanding. Also ask Him to make you aware of your gift(s). (See James 4:2.)

(3) *Awareness.* Become knowledgeable about what Scripture has to say about spiritual gifts.

(4) *Responsibility.* With spiritual gifts comes responsibility. So before you set out to discover your gift, you need to be willing to carry out the specific responsibilities that go with it. (See Acts 6:2-8; 8:6, 12-13; 21:8.)

(5) *Openness.* Open your heart and mind to what the Lord has for you. Don't fear or reject your gift out of your past experience or ignorance. You may need to pray this prayer of David: "Open my eyes that I may see wonderful things in Your law" (Ps. 119:18).

(6) *Confirmation.* Your desires, your experience, and the counsel of others all fit into the discovery process. Use these sources to confirm what God shows you regarding your spiritual gift(s).

Even though this session is only an introduction to a vital subject, hopefully you have been enlightened enough to begin to identify, exercise, and study your gift(s) further.

The Greek word for spiritual gifts, *charisma,* means that God gives you the desire and power to do His will. And the Greek derivative *charis* means joy. As you minister to students, you will experience minimum weariness and frustration and maximum effectiveness and fulfillment when you discover and begin to exercise your spiritual gift.

[Many of the concepts in this session were taken from an unpublished paper by Don Crossland entitled, "A Study of Spiritual Gifts."]

ACTION POINT ☐ Session 31

1. Study the following passages thoroughly, using the Bible study methods learned in Section 1.
   Romans 12:3-9
   Ephesians 4:11
   1 Corinthians 12:27-31
   1 Corinthians 12:7-11
   List the gifts in the appropriate column below.

2. Of the grace (motivation) gifts, which one do you think you have? Why?

3. List some ways you might exercise your motivation gift in your ministry to young people. Be specific.

4. Memorize 1 Corinthians 12:11. Continue your daily readings from Mark.

GRACE GIFTS (FOR MOTIVATION)	SERVICE GIFTS (FOR MINISTRY)	WORKING GIFTS (FOR MANIFESTATION)
Romans 12:6-8	Ephesians 4:11 1 Corinthians 12:28	1 Corinthians 12:7-11

SESSION 32
LEADING A STUDENT TO CHRIST

I would predict that almost everyone reading this session would say that he or she believes in evangelism and in the Great Commission. But in reality, many people just don't practice what they believe. Too few people are getting out to talk to lost students. Why? Two primary barriers surface again and again: (1) Fear—some people are afraid of rejection; and (2) Time—some people want to witness but they don't take the time to do it.

The time problem has already been discussed in Session 29. You know how to arrange your schedule around your priorities. (And you know that talking to people about Jesus Christ is a definite priority!)

BARRIER	EXPRESSION	SOLUTION
GUILT	"I've got too many things wrong in my life. I don't want to be a hypocrite."	Confession (Rom. 8:1; 1 John 1:9)
DOUBT	"I'm not sure about my own relationship with Christ. How can I tell others?"	Assurance (John 5:24; 1 John 5:11-13)
FAILURE	"I'm afraid I will fail."	Power of Holy Spirit (John 20:21-22)
APATHY	"I'm afraid to get too committed or overly involved."	Right motives (Mark 4:19)
OFFEN-SIVENESS	"I might invade someone else's privacy."	Concern (1 Thes. 2:8)
LACK OF KNOWL-EDGE	"I don't know what to say. What if someone asks me a question I can't answer?"	Discipleship (1 Peter 3:15-16)
REJEC-TION	"I'm afraid of what others will say about me."	Confidence in Christ (Col. 1:27-29)

But fear is a barrier that expresses itself in several different ways. A few fear-inspired excuses (and remedies) are included on the chart.

After you overcome your fears and readjust your schedule, you still need to gather several tools before you can effectively communicate Jesus Christ to students. Several necessary tools are listed below.

The Tools Needed

(1) Communication tool—One of the big questions in witnessing is, "How do I begin a conversation with a student?" The most important thing is to be a friend. Your conversation will flow easily if you show a genuine interest in a student's life. If you need help getting started, this acrostic will remind you of some basic discussion topics:

Family
Recreation
Interests
Education
Needs
Destiny

Another common question is, "How do I make a transition from talking about student interests to talking about Jesus Christ?" At an appropriate point in your conversation, ask something like, "Have you ever thought much about Jesus Christ?" or "Sometime, could I tell you how Jesus Christ has changed my life?" Those are simple questions. Ask God for the boldness to use them. Also try to memorize the chart at the end of this session on "How to Build a Friendship Bridge." Your conversations will flow naturally when you ask the right questions and make the right responses.

(2) Testimony tool—Your testimony is *your* story. No one can refute it. Review what you wrote in the *Action Point* of session 4 and use these guidelines to help you tell your story more effectively.

■ Your personal experience should catch and hold the listener's attention.
■ Keep it short and to the point.
■ Talk about you.
■ Give details; be specific.
■ Relive it as you tell it.
■ Be positive.
■ Be prepared. (Have your testimony clearly in your mind.)

(3) Gospel tool—After you have shared your testimony, ask, "Have you ever considered asking Jesus Christ into your life?" If the person answers yes, ask him, "May I take a few minutes to explain how that can happen to you?" If he agrees, explain the Gospel to him in simple terms. (One of the most effective ways to communicate the Gospel is to go through a short written explanation and let the person ask any questions he has. An excellent booklet entitled "The Facts of Life" has been designed for this very

purpose. Copies can be ordered from the publisher or Reach Out Ministries.)

(4) Invitation tool—When you have finished explaining the Gospel (or reading the booklet), ask: "Is there any reason why you would not want to receive Jesus Christ right now?" Be sensitive to the Holy Spirit and realize that a spiritual battle is going on inside that person. Pray for him as you talk. Most importantly, don't leave until you give that person the opportunity to pray with you to receive Christ. (But don't get hung up on whether or not the person receives Christ at that very moment. Remember that receiving Christ involves more than hearing the Gospel and saying a prayer. The person must be prepared to make a significant decision, and the preparation and timing are up to the Holy Spirit.)

(5) Follow-up tool—Immediate follow-up is essential to a new Christian's success in walking with Christ. New believers need love, nourishment, protection, and training. If possible, set an appointment for the *very next day,* even if it's only on the phone.

In your conversation the next day, talk about:

■ Your presentation—review it and see if he or she has any questions.

■ His decision—go over the prayer again and make sure he understands his commitment.

■ The assurance—read passages of Scripture together from the Bible.

■ The growth process (as outlined in the booklet).

■ The need to become involved in a local church.

A Personal Strategy

If a youth leader wants to train his students to be effective witnesses, personal witnessing must first be a reality in his own life. Therefore:

■ Set aside a specific time in your schedule each week for personal witnessing. This may be during or apart from your regular church outreach.

■ Develop a Prayer Triangle. This is a list of three students you are praying for daily with whom you want to share Jesus Christ. Set up a time to meet with each one.

■ Take a student with you for "on-the-job" training when you witness to others. Encourage that student to develop his own Prayer Triangle. When you have finished with your original Prayer Triangle, start meeting with the students on his list.

■ After the student has seen you share your faith, begin to let him share some of the responsibility. Begin by letting him share his testimony and gradually increase his role until he feels comfortable carrying the entire conversation and sharing the Gospel by himself.

(NOTE: If you feel that you need further training in this area, I suggest that you find someone who can witness and go out with him. Also check with your church about getting involved with or beginning an evangelism training program.)

ACTION POINT ☐ Session 32

1. What is your greatest barrier in witnessing? Why?

2. This week talk to a non-Christian student using the FRIEND acrostic. Report the results of that conversation below.

3. Write out your testimony using this outline:
   (1) How my life was before I met Christ
   (2) How I met Christ
   (3) How my life changed after I met Christ
   If you have already done this, try to sharpen what you wrote before.

4. Whom do you know who can show you how to witness if you aren't sure of yourself? Whom can you show how to witness if you already know how?

5. Develop your Prayer Triangle using the chart below. Insert the names of three students in the triangle (and the chart), and begin to pray for them regularly.

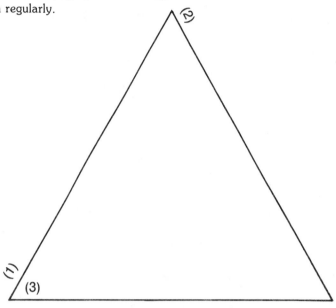

PRAYER TRIANGLE

DATE _____

NAME	SPIRITUAL CONDITION	ACTION I CAN TAKE	PRAYER REQUESTS	PERSON'S RESPONSE
1.				
2.				
3.				

6. Memorize Luke 19:10. Continue to have your times alone with God every day.

HOW TO BUILD
A FRIENDSHIP BRIDGE

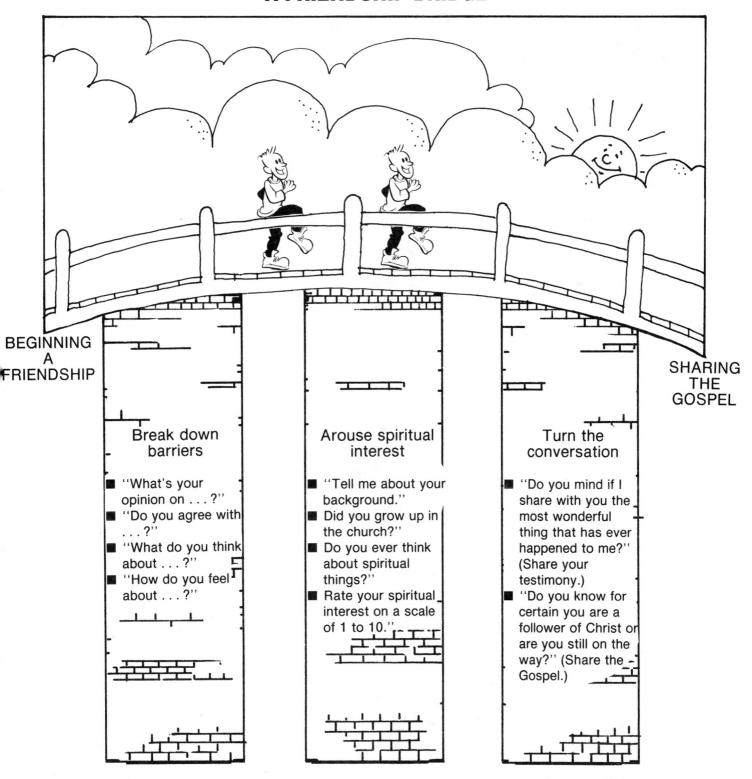

BEGINNING A FRIENDSHIP

SHARING THE GOSPEL

Break down barriers

- "What's your opinion on . . . ?"
- "Do you agree with . . . ?"
- "What do you think about . . . ?"
- "How do you feel about . . . ?"

Arouse spiritual interest

- "Tell me about your background."
- Did you grow up in the church?"
- Do you ever think about spiritual things?"
- Rate your spiritual interest on a scale of 1 to 10."

Turn the conversation

- "Do you mind if I share with you the most wonderful thing that has ever happened to me?" (Share your testimony.)
- "Do you know for certain you are a follower of Christ or are you still on the way?" (Share the Gospel.)

This bridge may be crossed in one meeting, or it could require a period of time.

SESSION 33
GROWING A NEW CHRISTIAN

Having babies is a life-changing experience! It not only includes the nine-month commitment of bringing them into the world. It also includes the lifetime process of nurturing them and watching them grow.

Producing spiritual "babies" requires the same long-lasting commitment. The Bible tells us that new believers, like "newborn babies, crave pure spiritual milk" (1 Peter 2:2). New Christians have certain needs that they can't meet for themselves. Like babies, they need "parents" who will meet their needs for love, nourishment, protection, and training.

Love—New converts need to know the security that results from being accepted and cared for. Communicating love is more than just talk; it includes action. Christ gave us the key to this when He said: "Love each other as I have loved you" (John 15:12). Jesus' love for His disciples was characterized by His willingness to give. If we are going to communicate His kind of love to new believers, we also must be willing to give—of our time, our resources, and ourselves. For a new believer, this kind of love begins with friendship, fellowship with other Christians, and the understanding of God's love and acceptance of him as His child.

Nourishment—New believers, like newborn babies, are totally dependent on someone else to feed them. It is as absurd to expect a new believer to feed himself as it is to expect a newborn baby to go into the kitchen and rustle up his own breakfast. Both are totally dependent on someone else to keep them fed and healthy. We become healthy when we are "brought up in the truths of the faith and of the good teaching" (1 Tim. 4:6).

Protection—Young Christians, babies, and sheep have a lot in common—when it comes to defending themselves, they're pretty helpless. New believers need to be protected because "the devil prowls around like a roaring lion looking for someone to devour" (1 Peter 5:8). Until young Christians become strong enough to handle Satan's attacks, they need someone who can help them learn how to live in the power of the Holy Spirit.

Training—Just as parents train their children for the challenges of life, spiritual parents must train their "children" to be "rooted and built up in Him, strengthened in the faith" (Col. 2:7). Young Christians need training in the basics: assurance that Christ lives in them, how to spend time with God in prayer and Bible study, the need for fellowship, how to share their faith, and living in obedience to Jesus Christ. New believers who have been nurtured in this way will have a good start on the road to maturity in Christ.

The Awesome Responsibility

Nurturing young Christians takes a lot of commitment, time, and preparation. So why should you even agree to take on such an awesome responsibility? I can think of at least four good reasons.

You were a part of their spiritual birth. Your job isn't finished when you have helped someone become a Christian. That person needs you to help him get established in the faith. A good example can be found in Acts 14:21-22. After preaching to the people, Paul took the time and responsibility to strengthen the new converts and exhort them to continue in the faith.

You have a responsibility as a member of the body of Christ. If you see a new believer who is not being cared for, your responsibility is to help him grow. Paul explains that the responsibility of *every* Christian is to equip the saints for the work of the ministry until we all attain mature manhood. We should no longer be children. Rather, we are to grow up in every way into Him who is the head. (See Eph. 4:11-16.)

You love Jesus. Our care for those who belong to Christ proves our love for Him. In John 21:15-17, Jesus told Peter to demonstrate his love for Him by feeding His sheep (caring for fellow Christians).

Jesus commanded it. Jesus instructs us to "make disciples of all nations" (Matt. 28:18-20). Notice His choice of words. He doesn't say we're to make "converts." We are to make "disciples"—people who are consistent followers of Jesus.

It is a tremendous privilege to take care of God's children. We can be a part of achieving His goal to "present everyone perfect [mature] in Christ" (Col. 1:28).

What to Do

Leading a person to Christ is important, but it's only the first step. The bigger challenge is helping him grow to maturity. But until they learn to walk by themselves, new Christians need your help. Spiritual parents must: (1) Be controlled by the Holy Spirit and sensitive to His leading, (2) Pray consistently that the new convert will grow to maturity in Christ, and (3) Be a friend.

Follow these guidelines when you are working with a new Christian:

(1) Meet with him immediately after he receives Christ. Studies show that a person who is contacted within 48 hours after becoming a Christian has a much easier time growing in his relationship with Christ.

(2) Meet with him at least four times after he becomes a Christian. (Use the formats at the end of this week's lesson for each meeting.)

(3) If he asks a question you can't answer, be honest. Say, "I don't know." Don't try to make up an answer. Tell him you will try to find the answer before you meet again.

(4) Don't get discouraged if the person does not respond as

you had expected. The growth process takes time. If you keep on loving, nourishing, protecting, and training the other person, growth *will* take place. Jesus said in the Parable of the Sower (Matt. 13) that some people would not grow after they received the Word, but that many others would grow by leaps and bounds. Your task is to follow up people in the power of the Holy Spirit and then let God take care of their response. Remember this: "So neither he who plants nor he who waters is anything, but only God, who makes things grow. The man who plants and the man who waters have one purpose, and each will be rewarded according to his own labor" (1 Cor. 3:7-8).

Remember, helping new Christians grow is one of the great adventures of being a Christian!

ACTION POINT ☐ Session 33

1. Study John 21:15-17 carefully and write down what you think is your role in feeding Jesus' "sheep."

2. Study the four follow-up sessions that follow. After you have read through all four lessons, write an outline for each lesson on a 3″ × 5″ card. You will use this when you meet with students for follow-up.

3. Think of one student you know who is a new or young believer. Set up an appointment with that student, and during the next four weeks, share each of the lessons on follow-up with him.

4. Memorize 1 Peter 2:2 and maintain your daily times alone with God and readings from Mark.

BEGINNING THE NEW LIFE
(Follow-up session #1 for a new Christian)

1. Begin with some friendly conversation.
2. Review the basic outline on how to receive Christ (preferably by using "The Facts of Life" booklet or other short, simple presentation).
3. Make sure that the new Christian understands that Christ is in his life. Read and explain: (1) 1 John 5:11-13—We can *know* that we have *life,* and (2) Romans 8:38-39—Nothing can separate us from God's love.
4. Ask: "What about feelings? What if you wake up some morning and just don't feel like Jesus is in your life? Does that mean He has left you?" Explain that Christians do not need to depend on feelings. The following diagram illustrates the relationship of fact (God and His Word), faith (our trust), and feeling (the result of trust). As Christians, our feelings should be controlled by our faith.

FACT—The chair can support a person's weight.   FAITH—The chair can support my weight.   FEELINGS—Comfort and security result because an action was taken by faith based on fact.

5. Read 2 Corinthians 5:17. Explain that a new Christian has begun a relationship so completely different that the New Testament calls it "new birth." Just as a newborn baby must grow physically, a new Christian must grow spiritually.
6. Discuss practical ways to grow in Christ. (The last pages of "The Facts of Life" booklet will also be helpful in this area.)
7. Ask if he has any questions and see if you can help him in any way.
8. Ask him to read Mark 1—4 and memorize 1 John 5:11-12 before you meet again.
9. After setting up a time to meet with him again, close in prayer.

CONFESSING SIN
(Follow-up session #2 for a new Christian)

1. After some friendly conversation, ask how things have been going since he received Christ. Be sensitive to his needs.
2. Ask: ''Are you confident that your past, present, and future sins are forgiven and that Christ is in your life?''
3. Explain to him that even though Christ will never leave him, it is easy for a Christian to take control of his own life and not let Christ control him. Emphasize that refusing to let Christ take control is a sin.
4. Explain that to get rid of the daily sins he commits, the Christian must confess those sins. Point out that sin can be an *attitude* (of indifference or rebellion toward God) as well as an *action.* Read 1 John 1:8-10 and explain that confession is agreeing with God concerning our sins. We agree that our sin is wrong and that Christ has forgiven us through His death. Confession does not make us any more forgiven, but it acknowledges our sin to God and expresses our gratitude for His forgiveness. Confession is the first thing a person must do to remain in a close fellowship with Christ.
5. Have him read Mark 5—8 for next time.
6. Set up a time when you can meet again and then pray together.

FILLING OF THE HOLY SPIRIT
(Follow-up session #3 for a new Christian)

1. After some friendly conversation, ask, ''How has the practice of confession helped you understand God's forgiveness?''
2. Explain that God wants to give us an abundant and exciting life. We live that life by the power of the Holy Spirit. Use the following verses to support your explanation: John 10:10; Acts 1:8; Galatians 5:22-23; and Ephesians 5:18.
3. Read Romans 8:9-11 and explain that the Holy Spirit lives in everyone who has received Christ. But even though the Holy Spirit lives in every believer, He does not control every Christian.
4. Explain that we are commanded to be controlled by the Holy Spirit, and read John 20:22. Ask, ''Would God command you to do something which was impossible for you to fulfill?''
5. Read 1 John 5:14-15 and explain how we can be filled with the Holy Spirit by asking God in faith. Pray with the new convert for the filling of the Holy Spirit.
6. Explain that a Christian may need to confess his sins and ask to be filled with the Holy Spirit many times in one day. By these two steps, confession and filling, a Christian can live life at its best. Illustrate by using the following comparison. Say something like: Physical breathing requires a simple two-step process. *Exhaling* removes impurities from your lungs. *Inhaling* brings in clear, pure oxygen. Spiritual breathing is similar. You *exhale* by confessing your sins (1 John 1:9). Then you *inhale* by claiming the filling of the Holy Spirit (Eph. 5:18). Explain to the new Christian how important it is to do this every day.
7. Ask him to read Mark 9—12 and to memorize Ephesians 5:18.
8. Set up a time when you can meet together next week and then pray together.

GETTING TO KNOW GOD
(Follow-up session #4 for a new Christian)

1. After some casual conversation, ask, "How has the practice of spiritual breathing helped you live the Christian life this week?"
2. Show him the wheel illustration and look up these verses as you explain each segment.

Christ the Center	(2 Cor. 5:17; Gal. 2:20)
Obedience to Christ	(John 14:21; Rom. 12:1)
The Word	(Josh. 1:8; 2 Tim. 3:16)
Prayer	(John 15:7; Phil. 4:6-7)
Fellowship	(Matt. 18:20; Heb. 10:24-25)
Witnessing	(Matt. 4:19; Rom. 1:16)

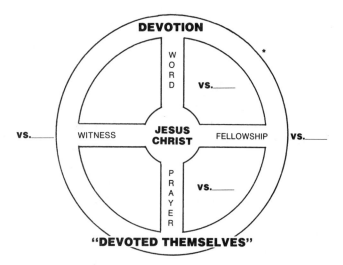

Help him to see the idea of *balance* in each of these areas and that he needs to obey the things he learns in each area.

3. Have him begin a daily time alone with God. Look at Philippians 3:10 to see what his goal should be. Look at Mark 1:35 to see who set the example. Look at Psalm 41:1-2 to see what his attitude should be. Then have a time alone with God together using what he has learned, a Bible Response Sheet (like the one in session 10), and a Prayer Action Sheet (like the one in session 12). First work through each step with the other person, using Galatians 2:20. Then do another one separately using 2 Corinthians 5:17. Make sure the application is personal, practical, and measurable.

4. Challenge him to have a time alone with God for ten straight days. Have him use one verse each day from the list in question #2.
5. Ask him to finish Mark (chapters 13—16) and to memorize Philippians 3:10.
6. Talk to him about being baptized and about becoming a member of your church and your youth group. Take him with you to visit.
7. Determine what the two of you need to do next. One suggestion is to get him into a discipleship group using *Following Jesus* (Barry St. Clair, Victor Books).
8. Pray together.
9. As a gift, give him a copy of the book, *The Big Man on Campus* (Barry St. Clair, Victor Books). Have him read it and let you know what he thinks.

SESSION 34
CHALLENGE FOR DISCIPLESHIP

After the youth meeting at your church, a high school freshman tells you, "I really want to be what God wants me to be, but I don't know what that is." How would you answer him?

Before you answer, dream a little. Imagine this student in terms of what he will be like as a senior. What qualities would he need to develop between now and then to become mature in his walk with Christ? Think about what he would be like if he developed all those qualities. Also try to imagine what you, as his leader, could do to help him become that kind of person.

The Discipled Student

Church activities, Bible studies, mission trips, special events, camps, and retreats are often planned with the hope that the students who participate will "turn out all right." But what does it mean to "turn out all right"? Let's be honest, if you don't have a clear definition in mind, it's very likely that you will always have an uneasy feeling that you haven't really done all you should to help a student.

The Bible gives us a clear definition of what it means to "turn out all right":

"Him we preach and proclaim, warning and admonishing everyone and instructing everyone in all wisdom, that we may present every person mature—full-grown, fully initiated, complete, and perfect—in Christ, the Anointed One. For this I labor, striving with all the superhuman energy which He so mightily enkindles and works within me (Col. 1:28-29, AMP).

Our struggle as youth workers is to teach and admonish students to become "mature in Christ." So let's get a clear picture of what a mature student would look like, defining *maturity* as coming to the point where we are able to receive enough from Jesus to meet our own needs *and* the needs of others.

Getting Started

Keep the following thoughts in mind as you think about helping students grow to such a level of maturity.

- Allow students to mature naturally. You can encourage them to grow, but you can't force them.
- You are building the foundation for a student to continue to grow to maturity throughout his life, so don't expect to see a final product on his graduation from high school. Do expect to see rapid growth toward becoming the type of person God wants him to be.
- Every activity in your church can be a tool to help students grow to maturity. Plan your programs with that in mind.
- Students grow to maturity in three environments: large groups, small groups, and one-to-one. Each environment has its place in a student's development.
- Realize that you are not the only resource to help students grow—parents, teachers, other church members, family, and friends are all influential. Consider how everyone can work together in this process.

Defining and Refining

To complete the process of defining a mature student, you will need to spend some time in reflection. Study God's Word, listen to Him, and think about the type of student you would like to see your youth ministry produce. Record your thoughts on the "Profile of a Disciple" sheet at the end of this session. As your Profile develops, use these steps to refine it.

- Make it realistic. Consider time limitations as well as maturity limitations. You will need to raise some standards and lower others. Always believe that God changes lives, but don't let your Profile exceed the limits of spiritual reality.
- Define clichés and vague words. The description of each quality needs to be understood by you and those who work with you.
- Make each quality practical and measurable. Offer a plan for a student to achieve each characteristic in the power of God's Spirit.
- Condense the Profile to one page so it will be easier to keep before you. Use it to help you gauge your progress and determine the activities that you want to include in your program. Having a one-page profile will also help you communicate your goals to others.

ACTION POINT □ Session 34

1. Study 1 Thessalonians 1 and define the qualities of a discipled student.

2. Study 1 Thessalonians 2 and define the desired qualities of a person who disciples students.

3. Think of one specific student you are currently discipling or are planning to start discipling. Analyze your personal goals for helping that student become a mature person in Christ by using the "Profile of a Disciple" sheet on the next page. You will want to use this format for each student you disciple to help you keep clearly in mind what you are trying to accomplish. It might be helpful to use some of the questions from your Profile of a Disciple on a questionnaire to give to each student. Combining his input with your plans will help you keep your goals for him practical and attainable.

4. After you complete your Profile, refine it on a regular basis. Consider the following areas you may have overlooked:
   ■ The desire to glorify God through his life (1 Cor. 10:31).
   ■ The desire to live a balanced personal life (Matt. 22:36-38).
   ■ The desire to relate positively to and take responsibility for his family (Eph. 6:4).
   ■ The desire to serve Jesus Christ with total abandonment both now and in the future (Prov. 3:5-6).

5. Memorize Colossians 1:28-29, and keep up your daily Bible readings. (If you've kept up with the suggested readings from the Check-Off Sheet in the Appendix, you should complete the Book of Mark this week!)

PROFILE OF A DISCIPLE*

PROFILE FOR _____ DATE_____
(Person's Name)

Study 1 Timothy 3:2-7; 1 Peter 5:1-7; Acts 6:3-5; and Titus 1:7-9. Using these passages of Scripture and 1 Thessalonians 1—2, answer the following questions. Identify at least one verse of Scripture for each of your answers.

What life goals should this person be committed to?

In what area(s) of this person's life should he (or she) be able to make his (or her) own decisions?

What characteristics should his (or her) life reflect spiritually, mentally, physically, and socially?

What kind of relationship should he (or she) have with his (or her) family (parents, brothers, sisters)?

What kind of relationship should he (or she) have with his (or her) friends?

What kind of dating standards should he (or she) have?

What future goals and direction should he (or she) have?

*Adapted from Dennis Miller at the National Convention on High School Discipleship, 1983.

SESSION 35
COUNSELING STUDENTS

Imagine that one of the students in your youth group calls you late at night. He is obviously upset as he begins to tell you about a fight he had with his dad. During the fight he became frustrated and angry, so he stomped out of his house and drove down to the local hangout to get a beer. He got drunk, tried to drive home, and skidded into a tree. As he talks, you can see that he is scared, confused, and very down on himself. How would you handle that situation? What would you say to him?

Let's look at some basic principles and practical suggestions on counseling students that will prepare us to help students who are going through crises, like this young man. Obviously, you can't learn all you need to know about counseling students in this one session. But you can begin to build a foundation. When you get into specific counseling situations, you will need further guidance.

The Purpose for Counseling
Jesus promised us that following Him would give us the fullest, most rewarding life possible (John 10:10). But He never promised that the Christian life would be easy. We will all experience difficulties from time to time. Some will seem impossible for us to walk through. And those situations are frequent for a teenager who is struggling through adolescence.

What most students are looking for when they come for counseling is *happiness*. ("Get me out of this mess so that I can be happy.") But God's goal is for us to be *holy*. ("How can I put Christ first?") Paul tells us that God desires for us to be "conformed to the likeness of His Son" (Rom. 8:29). Our goal as counselors is to help students grow into being like Christ so they will be holy *then* happy.

The Basic Needs of Students
Trying to counsel without understanding the basic needs of students is like patching up their problems with Band-Aids rather than getting to the root and defeating that problem forever. At the root of all student needs is a desire for *security* and *significance*.

In order to understand the needs of students, let's go back to the beginning—Adam and Eve. In the garden, Adam and Eve had *personal worth*. God provided for them in such a way that they were *significant* and *secure*. These two qualities were basic to their sense of personal worth. After the Fall, the security and the significance they had felt were taken away.

Remember the biblical account? They became afraid of God and blamed each other (insecurity). Then, when they were thrown out of the garden, they lost their sense of dignity (insignificance).

Problems develop when basic needs for significance and security are threatened. People try to resolve their needs in different ways. Look at the following responses and the results of each one.

RESPONSE	RESULT
Basic human needs met with Christ.	Significance; security
Highest human needs met without Christ.	Pride; pleasure
Basic human needs met without Christ.	Violence; immorality

Through counseling, then, our desire is to meet students' needs of significance and security by establishing their personal worth in Jesus Christ.

Helping Students Solve Problems
The Bible describes both the problems and the solutions to the problems with which students need help. Every student who comes to you for counseling ultimately has the same problem—*selfishness*. Paul calls this basic problem "the old self" (Eph. 4:22). When a student is lost, that "old self" is in control.

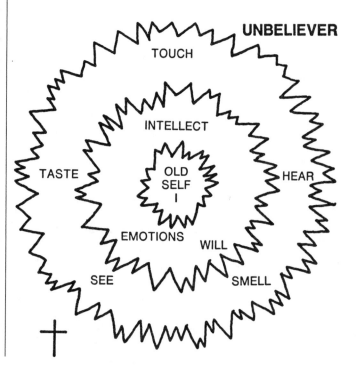

Because the old self is "corrupt," a person can never change until it is taken care of. So when you counsel students, the first step is *always* to help them determine if they know Jesus Christ. That leads them into a relationship that replaces their dependence on the old self (selfishness) with a dependence on Christ (significance and security).

Once the old self is removed from the center of power and the Holy Spirit comes and lives within his spirit (Rom. 8:9), a person has hope that he can change. Otherwise he will never be able to change.

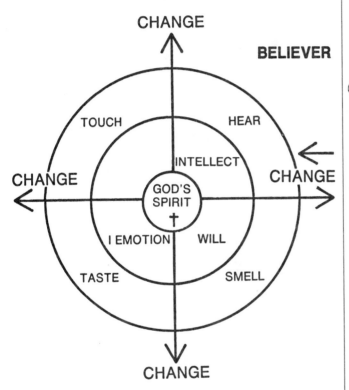

So when a student comes to you for counseling, you need to communicate to him that Jesus can reign in his life, making it possible for that student to change. If you don't get to the root problem (the old self), you are only putting Band-Aids on your students' problems.

Does all this mean that Christians should not have problems? No. Even though the old self is defeated, it still leaves behind a residue that continues to cause problems. We must help Christian students deal with those problems.

The Fruit and the Root

When students describe their problems, they almost always talk about the "fruit" of the problem—what is on the surface. If we deal with the fruit only, we will not help them. We must get to the "root." This is the hardest part of counseling. The root always comes out of the "old self." Whenever a student feeds the old self, it results in harmful effects on his life.

Let's go back to the student who says, "I got drunk and wrecked my dad's car." Getting drunk is only the fruit. The real solution is to look beyond the surface problem. Perhaps his dad puts him down, doesn't listen, and doesn't spend time with him. About 90 percent of the time, *rejection* is the root problem of today's young people. So try to work backward from the student's behavior until you discover his inner feelings. Here's an example.

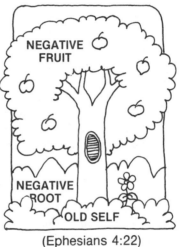

(Ephesians 4:22)

(1) Problem behavior "I got drunk and wrecked the car." (Loss of personal worth)
(2) Problem feelings "I can't do anything right when and where my dad's concerned." (Feelings of insignificance)
(3) Problem thoughts "My dad doesn't like me. If he did, he wouldn't yell at me and put me down. He would take time to get to know me." (Rejection)

Uprooting the Problem

Now that you see how to identify the problems, go back to Ephesians 4:22-24 to discover how to uproot the problems from students' lives. Verse 22 says to put off your old self with regard to your former manner of life. So help students *renounce* their sinful thoughts and actions. They do this by confession. Have them confess everything very specifically and thoroughly before you. Remind them that when they confess their sins to others, healing takes place (James 5:16). (Men should confess to men and women should confess to women. Have them confess discreetly, but specifically.) Using 1 John 1:9, show students that through their confession they are forgiven. Then have them make a contract right there to continue to put off the "old self."

After renouncing their sins, students need to be *renewed*. Ephesians 4:23 tells us to be made new in the attitude of our minds. Here are some practical ways to help students *renounce* their old actions and become *renewed*.

1. *Teach them to recognize their thoughts.* Challenge them to be honest and admit it when a wrong thought creeps into their minds. This is the first step toward solving the problem.

2. *Teach them to refuse wrong thoughts.* Suggest that when a wrong thought comes into their minds, that they quickly bring it before the Lord and confess it honestly.

3. *Teach them to replace their thoughts.* Show them from Scripture how that problem should be dealt with, then have them memorize a helpful verse. For example, if a student is having problems with feeling rejected by his parent(s), you might show him John 15:16 and explain that God never rejects him. Then go to Colossians 3:20 to show him how he should respond to his dad. Have him memorize one of those verses. (You will need to know your Bible. If you don't know the solution from Scripture, go to your pastor or youth minister and ask for help. Then get back to the student as soon as possible.)

4. *Teach them to reflect on their thoughts.* Encourage students to meditate on Scripture until it becomes like a surgeon's scalpel, cutting everything out of their minds that doesn't belong there. Encourage them to turn their minds to some positive thought every time a negative thought begins to emerge. Teach them to concentrate on "whatever is true, whatever is noble, whatever is right, whatever is pure, whatever is lovely, whatever is admirable . . . excellent or praiseworthy" (Phil. 4:8).

So in counseling you start with problem behavior (fruit) and work backward to discover the root problem (thoughts influenced by the old self). When the root is replaced with the new self, the change results in positive behavior. In turn, that positive behavior results in positive feelings.

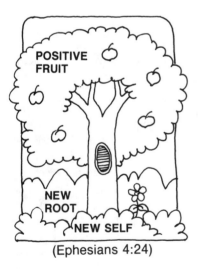

(Ephesians 4:24)

(3) Positive behavior
    "True righteousness
    and holiness"—
    Ephesians 4:24
    (Personal worth)
(2) Positive feelings
    "Put on the new self,
    created to be like
    God"—Ephesians 4:24
    (Significance and
    security)
(1) Positive thoughts
    "Be made new in the
    attitude of your minds"
    —Ephesians 4:23
    (Renewed mind)

Counseling students is not easy, but when you get to the root of the problems and then uproot them with biblical solutions— always pointing to Jesus who gives personal worth—then you will find that deep change will take place in the lives of your students.

ACTION POINT ☐ Session 35

1. Who is one person you would trust as a counselor in your church?

2. Write down the name of one student you work with who has an unsolved problem.

   What is the "fruit" issue that he is dealing with?

   Using the tree diagram, trace the student's problem from the fruit to the root of the issue.

   Outline the solution you would give to that student to solve his problem.

3. Discuss the information in question #2 with your youth minister or the person you listed under question #1.

4. Call the student you listed in question #2 and ask if you could meet with him or her this week. In your appointment, if the situation allows for it, gently approach the person's problem and talk through the "fruit" and the "root." If the student is still open, discuss your suggestions with him.

5. Record the result of your meeting with that student here.

6. Memorize Ephesians 4:22-24.

7. Continue to have time alone with God each day. If you have completed the Book of Mark, begin another book of the Bible or select passages each day that will be meaningful to you. You're on your own now, so don't give up! (If you have slipped behind in your readings from Mark, use this week and next week to catch up.)

SESSION 36
LEADING A SMALL GROUP

You walk into a Sunday School class or a small group you are leading. As you begin, you notice the students aren't paying any attention. How can you convert that apathetic group into a group interested in discussing significant issues?

As Jesus began to initiate His plan to change the world, He spent a great deal of time pouring His life into a band of twelve men. He befriended them, shared His heart and life with them, and challenged them to follow Him. He used a variety of methods and situations to slowly develop their spiritual understanding.

Spending time with these men was a priority in Jesus' ministry. Yes, He did evangelize the multitudes, but He also set aside special time for His chosen disciples. It was to this small group of individuals that Jesus later said: "Go into all the world and preach the Good News to all creation" (Mark 16:15). And those men, united by a common purpose and encouraged by a common love, were greatly used by God to change the course of human history.

The New Testament tells us that we, as fellow believers, are to do several things: bear each other's burdens (Gal. 6:2); encourage each other (Heb. 10:24-25); be concerned for each other (Phil. 2:4); and admonish each other (1 Thes. 5:15). The open, honest sharing that is necessary for this kind of ministry to take place is seldom achieved in large-group meetings. Jesus knew that to develop faithful, committed, spiritually mature disciples, He needed a small-group setting that would encourage close fellowship.

The use of small groups is no less powerful today than it was in the days of Jesus and the apostles. When these life-encouraging small groups are present and functioning correctly, a deep and moving fellowship is felt within the church.

Essential Principles

Let's begin to learn how we can have effective small groups. Here are some basic principles.

Establish the purpose of the group. When Jesus called His disciples, He did so with two basic purposes in mind: (1) to be "followers" who would imitate Him, and (2) to become "fishers of men" (Mark 1:16-17). As you recruit people to be part of your small group, keep these two purposes in mind.

Expect great things. Great things don't usually happen within a group unless the leader keeps the end result constantly before the others so that they keep moving in the right direction. People are a lot like sheep—without good direction, they will wander. We need to have God's purpose for our group clearly in mind and then direct the group toward that goal. Remember that the Holy Spirit is the true leader. Expect Him to give the group power and purpose.

Encourage group members. When His disciples became confused, Jesus took them aside and tried to explain what He was doing. When they were joyous, He rejoiced with them. When they were down, He reassured them. Small groups are great for encouragement. "Two are better than one, because they have a good return for their work: if one falls down, his friend can help him up. But pity the man who falls and has no one to help him up! (Ecc. 4:9-10)

Preparing for the Group Meeting

Small groups don't just happen. You must prepare for their success. Here are some basics to consider.

Prepare with individuals of the group in mind. As you get ready for the group, pray for potential members by name, remembering their individual needs. Ask yourself, "How does this relate to Jim, Sue, and John? How can I communicate to them most effectively?"

Prepare in detail. Make sure you write out your plans. Plan each meeting minute by minute, so your time will not be wasted or misused. Also consider the physical setting and try to create a good atmosphere for your group.

Prepare by personalizing. Make sure your students know you care for them as specific individuals, not just an undefined "group." Your warmth, communicated as they come in, makes a great deal of difference. Rather than feeling awkward or intimidated, people will feel welcome.

Prepare to stay within a time frame. The meeting needs to last at least an hour, but not more than two. Keep a close watch on time. Make the most of the time you have, but never go over your designated time limitations.

During the Group Meeting

After you begin your meetings, here are some goals to keep in mind.

Encourage group members to be honest. Lead by example. Students will only be as honest and open as you are—so share your weaknesses, your failures, and your hurts as well as your positive anecdotes and examples.

Be aware of individual needs. It is important for group members to support each other. But if someone is really hurting (and taking up a lot of the group's time), that person should be sensitive to the rest of the group. You may want to ask the individual if you and he can get together after the meeting. Then you are free to move ahead with the group.

Give group members "practical handles." Each session should contain something that will help students apply what they are learning. For example, if you are discussing spending time alone with God, give specific illustrations of how you spend time alone with God, what you do during your prayertimes, or how you meditate on Scripture. Walk them through any steps they aren't familiar with.

The Process of the Group

In baseball, the idea is to get a hit and then move around the bases to score. In leading a small group, we have the same challenge—to successfully move through a series of steps until the individuals and the group are making significant decisions concerning their relationships with Jesus Christ. This diagram explains the process.

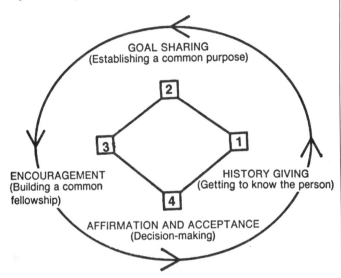

Building Strong Personal Relationships in the Group

You want your group to be spiritually mature, but you also want them to be friends with each other. Below are some ideas to help establish strong friendships.

Establish group goals and commitments. One good definition of *friendship* is "sharing common experiences built around common goals." As you begin to see goals reached and commitments kept, you will also see friendships begin to blossom.

Spend time together socially. Do fun things together as a group. Also spend time with the individuals in your group by participating in their social activities, taking them with you while you run errands, and so forth.

Be the initiator. Ask group members questions about themselves, their interests, and their activities. Share those same things about yourself. Stay current with upcoming events and activities. Demonstrate your unconditional acceptance of them—be a friend first and a group leader second.

Sit close together. Check the physical arrangement of your meeting room. The closer you can get to having your knees touching, the more closeness you will feel within the group.

Observe body language. When people fold their arms, cross

their legs, slouch, turn away, or roll their eyes, they're giving nonverbal indications that they have lost interest. By the same token, when they are sitting forward in their chairs and keeping good eye contact, that shows that they are tuned in. Be aware of body language and adjust your teaching methods accordingly.

Dangers to Avoid

As your small groups are begun or developed, here are some things to try to avoid.

Don't become a clique. Small groups usually develop close friendships, but a healthy group will reach out to others. Even though your discipleship group may not be open to new members, your students can bring other friends to youth group activities.

Don't worry. After the initial excitement of a new group wears off, group members may go through a period of indifference. You can overcome this by allowing group members to share their feelings during a brief time of evaluation. Ask the group how things are going and encourage both positive and negative feedback. See what they think can be done to improve.

Don't panic. If you come up against a problem you don't feel equipped to handle, tell your group, "I have to give some thought to that and get back with you later." Then consult your youth minister (or someone else you feel can handle the problem) for an answer.

Leading a small group will be one of the most challenging, yet rewarding experiences you will ever have. The friendships you will cultivate and the changes you will see take place in the lives of your group members will give you a tremendous sense of satisfaction and joy.

ACTION POINT ☐ Session 36

1. If you are leading a small group, pick out the five suggestions from this session that you feel would be most helpful to you. Record them here.

If you are not leading a small group, prepare an outline to help start and lead your own small group. Then you will be ready when your opportunity comes.

Implement those suggestions in your small group this week. Record the results below.

2. Review the material in this session (and previous sessions). What things are you doing right as a leader?

What are some things you need to work on?

3. Memorize Hebrews 10:24-25 and faithfully continue to spend time alone with God in prayer and Bible study every day.

Appendix

☐ INSTRUCTIONS FOR GROUP LEADERS

Successful Leadership

During the next 36 weeks, you and everyone in your group will be growing. Growth depends on change, so you need to be flexible as your group members begin to face their own needs and the overall needs of your youth ministry. Be sensitive to the leading of the Holy Spirit as you oversee this study. You want to challenge each member to become equipped to handle any situation as he leads students to maturity in Christ. But as you assign youth ministry responsibilities to individual group members, be aware that some people will "take charge" more quickly than others. Get them involved when you see they are ready, but don't intimidate them.

Commitment is the key to a successful group study of this book. Limit the group to those adults who will commit themselves to study the book and Bible on their own, and who will faithfully take part in every group meeting and project. This group will be referred to as a Leadership Family.

It is good if the leader of the Leadership Family is the person in charge of working with youth in his church. If you're not, make sure that you have permission from the proper authority in your church to put together this group.

Being the leader of a Leadership Family will require more time and personal involvement than most Bible studies or Sunday School classes you may have taught in the past. As a member of the group (not just its leader), you should take part in all of the commitments, activities, and assignments of the Leadership Family. Here are some things you will need to do to get started.

Look through the material in this book. Examine the Table of Contents to get an overview of what you will be discussing, and then take a close look at several individual sessions to get a feel for the depth of the material and the level of commitment that will be required. Finally, become familiar with the purpose of each of the three sections and be ready to summarize them for the other group members.

Decide on a place and time to meet. You will be meeting weekly as a group throughout this study. At the first meeting everyone should decide on the best time for the group to meet. If possible, plan to hold the meetings in your home or the home of one of the group members. Meeting in the informal atmosphere of a living room or around a dining room table will help people open up and join in discussions.

Order all materials prior to the first meeting. Each participants of the Leadership Family (including yourself) will need a Bible, a copy of *Building Leaders for Strategic Youth Ministry*, and a 5½" x 8½" binder for the *Time Alone With God Notebook Inserts.* (The inserts won't be introduced until *Week 9.*)

Set a maximum of two hours for each meeting. Shoot for 1½

hours each week: (15 minutes for review or sharing, one hour for the main study, and 15 minutes of prayer for personal needs). The order of activities is flexible as long as all three elements are included in every session.

Building Relationships

Your role in the Leadership Family is that of leader, not teacher. By explaining that you too are in the process of becoming a more mature disciple of Christ, you will establish yourself as one of the group, rather than as the "instructor." But expect group members to look to you for organization, guidance, and example. When they begin to see that you genuinely love God and that you care about them as individuals, they will form solid, loving relationships with God, with you, and with one another. Here are some suggestions for building stronger relationships:

1. *Meet with each group member.* Schedule an appointment with each person in your Leadership Family during the first week or two. Get to know his needs, interests, concerns, and goals. Share those same things about yourself. This will help you see one another as unique, important individuals with feelings and ideas. It will also result in more meaningful discussions during your group meetings.

2. *Keep a notebook throughout this study.* Record your observations about the members of your Leadership Family. Regularly pray for each person by name. Keep track of individual needs and achievements. If someone misses a session, contact him personally. Help him when he has trouble understanding something from Scripture. Talk with him if he seems to be neglecting his commitments. Ask his opinions during meetings. Build each member up so he will feel valued and appreciated by the rest of the group.

3. *Keep your pastor and church informed.* While you're building relationships in your Leadership Family, strengthen relationships within your church as well. Keep your pastor informed about what is happening in your group. Encourage group members to be involved in the church and to strengthen their relationships with other believers—especially the young people in your church.

4. *Limit group membership.* Because your Leadership Family will be building trust based on shared experiences, don't add any new members once the group has been established. (As new people become interested in joining, start a new Leadership Family for them at a later date.)

Establishing Session Leaders

Part of the learning experience of this group will come from the opportunity of each member to lead several Leadership Family meetings. A weekly schedule of meetings is on page 121. You should make assignments during the first week of each Section. (Only assign those weeks that are blank.) Assign leadership randomly, not based on expertise.

Have the leader for each session read the material under "Preparing to Lead" the *day after* the previous group meeting.

☐ PREPARING TO LEAD

1. *Prepare early.*
   Begin your preparation for leading the session at least *five days* prior to the group meeting. Study the material in this book, and answer the questions for yourself as a participant, not as you think others might answer. Read through the Discussion Guide to see if there is anything you need to do right away. After reviewing the session material and studying the discussion ideas, finalize your preparation one or two days before the meeting.

2. *Start on time.*
   Since Leadership Family meetings can last up to two hours, make sure that you take the initiative in getting the meetings started on time.

3. *Keep discussion on track:*
   - State questions clearly and concisely. After you ask a question, allow time for the group to think. Don't be afraid of short periods of silence. Don't jump in with your own answers or opinions. Don't make a contribution to the discussion that someone else in the group can make.
   - Respect each person's comments. Encourage everyone to say what he really thinks rather than what he thinks he should say. Ask additional questions to help him clarify his thoughts and move from ideas to application.
   - Stay close to Scripture. The Bible is the authority for this study and your group discussions. Encourage group members to base their ideas on biblical principles.
   - Challenge trite or superficial answers. Don't let group members get away with simply rattling off a cliché or a Bible verse. Ask them to explain what they mean and give illustrations wherever possible.
   - Ask review questions. Help the group think through new concepts in relation to previous studies. Use review times for members to raise previously discussed issues with which they are still having problems.
   - Make sure everyone participates. If some group members are hesitant to take part in the discussions, ask them direct questions relating to their personal opinions or experiences. Let them know that you care about them and what they think. If some members try to answer all the questions, begin addressing your questions to others by name so everyone will have an opportunity to respond.

4. *Evaluate every session.* Within 24 hours of each meeting, review how the session went. Talk with the Group Leader about any problems or needs you noticed in the group. Also ask him to point out your strengths and weaknesses so you can improve your leadership abilities.

SESSION	SECTION ONE	SESSION	SECTION TWO	SESSION	SECTION THREE
1	Group Leader	13	Group Leader	25	Group Leader
2	Group Leader	14	Group Leader	26	Group Leader
3	Group Leader	15	_____	27	Group Leader
4	Group Leader	16	_____	28	_____
5	Group Leader	17	_____	29	_____
6	Group Leader	18	_____	30	Group Leader
7	_____	19	_____	31	_____
8	_____	20	_____	32	_____
9	_____	21	_____	33	_____
10	_____	22	_____	34	_____
11	_____	23	_____	35	_____
12	_____	24	_____	36	_____

DISCUSSION GUIDES

If you are assigned to lead a session, use the appropriate discussion guide to help you get started. These questions and suggestions will help you get to the heart of each session. (These guides are by no means exhaustive, so add your own questions, ideas, and applications as well.)

Session 1 (Group Project)

1. During this first session, you will want to build relationships and organize your group. Make sure this meeting is informal and fun. Try to plan a picnic, bike hike, a party at someone's house, or a visit to some other local point of interest. At an appropriate time, gather your group members and ask each person to talk about himself (past, present, and future) for one minute. Then have each person describe what he wants to get (and to offer the other members) from participating in this group. Discuss what will be expected of each member of the Leadership Family (completion of all assignments, commitment to attend group meetings, willingness to apply what is learned, etc.).

2. Discuss: **Why do you want to be in the Leadership Family? What do you expect to get out of it? What might you have to give up to follow through on your commitments?**

3. If potential group members do not yet have copies of *Building Leaders*, try to hand out copies at this meeting. Let the group members take home a copy, look through it, and read and complete session 2 if they wish to commit themselves to the group. If someone doesn't wish to be part of the group, have him return his unmarked copy to you during the next week. (Gently question him to see why he doesn't wish to continue. Make sure he isn't dropping out because of fear, lack of self-esteem, or any of the other hesitations that will be covered in future sessions.)

4. Set a date and time for the next meeting, and make that your regular time to meet each week.

Session 2

1. Ask each person to take two minutes to tell as much about himself as possible (family, goals, dreams, job, etc.). Time each participant to insure that each person receives an equal amount of time.

2. Review the story about the Communist party leader and the statement that every follower of Jesus Christ is a potential leader in the faith. Ask: **Do you see yourself as a potential leader? Why?** Let each person respond.

3. Ask: **Which of the benefits of leadership are most meaningful to you?**

4. Ask someone in the group to read the material under

the subhead, "The Commitment to Leadership." Discuss commitment in terms of being in a group. Have each group member sign the "Personal Commitment" statement of all the other members. Explain that this is a sign of the commitment group members will have to each other.

5. Let everyone give a *brief* description of his schedule. Check to see if anyone expects problems in attending the group meetings every week. (If so, have those people talk to you after the meeting. Perhaps you can arrange for a baby-sitter for the group, meet on a different night, etc.).

6. Pray about the commitment each member has made to being in the Leadership Family.

7. Set a date now for your half day of prayer. (See Session 13.)

Session 3

1. Have each participant share his "favorite hobby" to begin the meeting.

2. Ask: **What are your reactions to the story about Matt Brinkley? Do you think God could ever bring about similar results in your personal life and ministry?**

3. Divide the group into pairs. Have everyone read the parable from Matthew 7:24-27 and talk about what truths they think Jesus is trying to communicate to us through the parable. As a group, create a modern-day parable that would communicate the same message.

4. Discuss the Alan Redpath quote. (See *Action Point* question #1.) What does it mean to your group of potential leaders?

5. Have each participant share his goals for this study. (Leader: Take notes to help hold group members accountable later.)

Session 4

1. Have each group member share his own "confidence in Christ"—how he came to know Jesus personally. (You may not want to open with personal testimonies, but be sure you allow plenty of time for them.)

2. Discuss situations where your group members tend to depend on feelings rather than facts in their personal relationships with Christ.

3. Review Psalm 139:13-16 and Ephesians 2:10. Ask: **Why do you think God created you?**

4. Review 1 John 4:9-10 and discuss how much God loves your group members. Have each person list one specific way that God cares for him.

5. Have group members discuss their lives "before" and "after" the presence of Christ. Look up as many passages (listed in the session) as time permits and summarize each one.

6. Discuss group members' answers to the question: "How do I know I have truly become a child of God?" What other evidence can they think of besides what they discovered in 1 John?

Session 5

1. Discuss common misconceptions about love.
2. Ask: **What is your fondest memory of experiencing love?**
3. Ask: **Of the four ways man's love and God's love differ, which one has affected you the most? Why?**
4. From their study of 1 Corinthians 13, have each group member pick out the quality of God's love that is most significant to him and tell the group why.
5. Have each member share one negative experience with love that has hampered him from receiving God's love.
6. Ask: **How will receiving God's love affect how you react to the three people you listed (in *Action Point* question #4)?**
7. Close with a prayer that each person will allow God's love to flow through him, cleanse him from past negative experiences with love, and help him love others more completely.

Session 6

1. Have group members share the one time in their lives when they felt the most inadequate.
2. Break down into groups of two. Have each pair read Psalm 51 and answer these questions: **Why was David feeling inadequate?** (His sin with Bathsheba. See 2 Samuel 11.) **How did David respond to God after his sin?** Get back together, have each group report their findings, and discuss each question.
3. Read 1 Timothy 1:5. Ask: **After reflecting on Paul's words to Timothy this week, what step of action did you realize you need to take in order to have a pure heart, good conscience, and sincere faith?** Encourage everyone to be specific. Then summarize: **Let's pray together and hold each other accountable for taking action by *next week.***

Session 7

1. Review the last session by discussing the action each individual was supposed to take as a result of his study of 1 Timothy 1:5. If some group members failed to complete their actions, let them know (in a positive way) that the rest of the group will continue to hold them accountable until action is taken. Let volunteers describe how they feel as a

result of being obedient to the Lord through their specific actions.
2. Have the group divide into pairs to read and discuss Romans 8. Have each pair list any characteristics that should be true of Christians. Then ask them to consider how those ideal characteristics should affect our actions. Reassemble and let each pair share their list of characteristics and their thoughts.
3. Ask volunteers to share what they think it means to "walk in the Spirit." Discuss this concept as a group. *Be practical.*
4. As the leader, share one example from your own personal life where you are (or have been) frustrated by circumstances or your inability to do what is right. Describe how walking in the Spirit might apply specifically to that area.
5. Let volunteers share some experiences where God has enabled them to keep from getting frustrated during trying circumstances.
6. Ask for specific prayer requests and then pray as a group. (You may want to try sentence prayer. Let someone begin with *one* sentence about a specific subject, and then other people can also pray *one* sentence about the same subject. Then move to another subject). Remind each person to pray that he will be filled with the Spirit and walk in the Spirit this week.

Session 8

1. Ask: **What is your favorite food and why?**
2. Read and discuss Colossians 2:6-10 together. Ask: **How did you receive Jesus Christ?** (through faith) **How can you walk in Him?** (also through faith) **How can you become rooted and built up in the faith, strengthened, and overflowing with thanks?** (Discuss responses.) **What are some of the "deceptive philosophies" and "human traditions" that keep us from experiencing fullness of life in Christ?** (secular humanism, church traditions, etc.) **How do those things affect us personally?** (opinion) **What do you think Paul means by "fullness of life in Christ?"**
3. Challenge your group members to use their "utensils" regularly (prayer, God's Word, fellowship, and witnessing). If some members are not in the habit of spending time alone with God every day, encourage them to begin this week. (You may want to have available copies of *Time Alone with God Notebook Inserts* for everyone. Spend as much time explaining the front sections of the inserts as you think your group members need. Emphasize the sections on "How to Have a Time Alone with God" and "How to Study a Passage of Scripture.") Point out that the next session will provide more specifics for beginning a daily time alone with God.

4. Remind your group members of the half day of prayer and begin to gather the materials you will need.

Session 9

1. Let each group member describe his or her first date.
2. Read Mark 1:35 as a group and discuss why Jesus needed to get off by Himself with His Father. (Emphasize that good relationships are maintained by spending time together.)
3. Have group members describe the most meaningful experience they have had while alone with God.
4. Ask: **How do you think spending time alone with God will help you achieve the goals you have set for this study?**
5. Discuss any questions group members might have about beginning a time alone with God.
6. Set a goal for every group member to spend time alone with God ten days in a row. If one or more persons miss a day during that period, agree to start over on the goal. This exercise should build unity and mutual encouragement to spend time alone with God. Emphasize honesty, because it won't hurt the group to start over one or more times. (You may want to call each group member sometime during the week to ask how he's coming with the group goal.)

Session 10

1. Ask: **What is one thing about your physical appearance that has changed since high school that people might comment on at a reunion?**
2. Brainstorm characteristics that the world sees as qualities of success. Then divide into groups of three and have each group write their own definition of success according to Psalm 1:1-3. Reassemble, share those definitions, and discuss how they differ from the world's ideas of success.
3. Have group members share insights from their times alone with God during the past week. Also have them share problems they faced.
4. As a group, work through each step of a Bible Response Sheet using Hebrews 4:12 as the passage. Then have group members individually work through another Bible Response Sheet, this time based on 2 Timothy 3:14-17. When everyone finishes, discuss each point. (This exercise should be more to help group members understand the *method* of Bible study than to gather a lot of insights from Scripture. First determine any problems they are having with filling out the Bible Response Sheet, and the insights will come naturally during their future times alone with God.)
5. Check to see how your group did on their 10-day commitment from last session. If anyone forgot or neglected to have a time alone with God (even for a day), designate the day after your meeting as "Day 1" and begin your 10-day

goal again. If everyone followed through with their times with God, have them continue to have a time alone with God every day during this study.

(Note: Ask group members to bring their Time Alone with God Notebooks to the next meeting.)

Session 11

1. Have each group member describe the most positive benefit of memorizing Scripture he has experienced or the obstacles that have prevented him from memorizing Scripture.
2. As a group, recite 2 Timothy 3:16. (Group members should have memorized this verse during the week.)
3. Using "How to Memorize Scripture" from the *Time Alone with God Notebook Inserts,* go over the steps of Scripture memory. Then memorize Hebrews 4:12 together.
4. Assign each person in the group one of the following verses to memorize on his own by using the steps of Scripture memory. Reassemble after a few minutes and have each person say his verse. Notice people who are having problems and make a mental note to call, encourage, and work with them if necessary to help them learn the verses. (Verses to Assign: 1 John 5:11; Philippians 1:6; 1 John 3:23; John 15:5; Psalm 119:9; John 16:24; Matthew 4:19; Proverbs 3:5-6; and Matthew 6:33.)
5. Read and discuss John 14:26 and 2 Peter 1:3. How might these verses relate to Scripture memory?
6. Have group members share from their personal times alone with God. (Check again to see how they are doing on ten straight days.) Pray for specific problems or insights they encounter.
7. Begin to finalize plans for the half day of prayer. (See Session 13.)

Session 12

1. Ask: **Do you consider yourself an "early bird" or a "night owl"? Why?** Pair up an early bird with a night owl as partners for encouragement in their times alone with God.
2. Have group members share insights from their times alone with God. (Celebrate if the group has completed its 10-day challenge.)
3. Discuss the purpose of prayer based on John 14:12-14 and Matthew 18:18-20.
4. Have each member share a recent specific answer to prayer (yes, no, or wait).
5. Break into groups and assign one aspect of prayer (praise, confession, thanksgiving, petition, intercession) to each group. Have groups define and tell *why* that aspect is so vital to a relationship with God. Reassemble and report.
6. Go over the sample Prayer Action Sheet. Make sure each

group member understands how every section applies to spending time in prayer.

7. Make sure everyone knows exactly what to do for next session's half day of prayer.

Session 13 (Group Project)

1. Contact each group member prior to this special meeting to confirm that he is planning to attend.

2. Gather individual prayer requests ahead of time and make copies (with the individual's permission) to hand out at the half day of prayer. Group members can pray for these requests during their "Prayer for Others" time.

3. Write a set of evaluation questions to use when your group reassembles after the half day of prayer. ("Was this a beneficial experience?" "If so, what prevents us from having in-depth prayer more often?" "How can we do this regularly?" etc.)

4. Gather materials that might be beneficial to group members during their half day of prayer. (See the list in Session 13 for suggestions.) Also try to collect lists of the young people in your church, other youth leaders, teachers and coaches at local schools, etc.

Session 14

1. Have everyone write down and then share with the group three major things they have learned as a result of their study of *Building Leaders* so far.

2. Divide into four groups and have each group study one of the first four chapters of Mark. Then reassemble and report on the principles Jesus used in His ministry.

3. Review aloud the five basic elements of the Reach Out Strategy. Be brief. Have each person report on where he or she is right now and where he would like to be in the future with regard to the Reach Out Strategy.

4. As a group, select one student listed under *Action Point* question #3. Discuss steps that could take that student from where he is right now to the point where he is a spiritual leader in your youth group. (Think back over the last thirteen sessions in your Leadership Family and what you have learned about leadership.) Discuss: **Is our youth ministry able to produce that kind of student?**

Session 15

1. Discuss: **What is one thing you do well? How did you get to be good at it?** (Tie this discussion to the fact that it takes time to develop a "good" Christian lifestyle.)

2. Divide into three groups and assign each group one of the following passages:
   Colossians 1:15-16

Hebrews 4:15
1 Corinthians 6:19-20
Reassemble and ask groups to report on their discussion.

3. Have everyone study Acts 22:1-16 on their own. Say: **As you consider the lordship of Christ in your life, how do you think Jesus would answer if you asked, "What shall I do, Lord?"** Discuss group members' answers.

4. As a group, read and discuss Philippians 2:9-11. Discuss: **Do you give Jesus enough respect in your life?** After the discussion, say: **Before you can go any deeper in your spiritual life, and before we can move ahead as a ministry team, each person must settle this issue of lordship.**

5. Close the meeting by having each person pray that the person on his right will completely commit himself to serve Jesus as Lord.

Session 16

1. Have each person share one funny or wild New Year's Resolution that he has made in the past but hasn't kept.

2. Discuss as a group the practical steps that Paul gives in Romans 12:1-2 toward making Jesus Lord of your life.

3. Read Matthew 16:24-26 and discuss the following questions: **What does it mean to deny yourself? What does it mean to take up your cross? What does it mean to follow Jesus? What did Jesus mean when He said, "Whoever wants to save his life will lose it, but whoever loses his life for Me will save it"? Why is it more important to have Jesus as your Lord than to gain the whole world?**

4. Have each person express one specific prayer request concerning the lordship of Christ in his life that the other group members can pray for. You may want to have everyone write their requests on cards and then exchange cards. Pray as a group for the requests that are shared.

[Note to Leader: This week can be a turning point for your group. If the group members try to continue without Jesus as Lord of their lives, their lack of commitment will be detrimental to themselves *and* the group. Challenge anyone who feels that he cannot make a commitment to Christ's lordship to talk it over with you during the next week.]

Session 17

1. Give everyone a paper plate and some markers. Have each person draw a composite picture of the average youth worker and then interpret his drawing for the group.

2. Discuss how members can build their levels of confidence as leaders by taking the approach Jesus took. (See John 8:29.)

3. Discuss John 13:1-10 and note how Jesus displayed vulnerability as a leader. Have the group come up with some ways to respond to others in a similar manner.
4. Assign each group member to befriend one student in your church and meet with him this week. Let each person select a student and explain why he wants to meet with that particular young person.

Session 18

1. Have each member share a time when he felt inadequate as a leader.
2. Say: **Peter had many weaknesses but he became one of the world's greatest leaders.** Discuss as a group the transformation of Peter from his first confrontation with Jesus until he became a powerful leader in Acts 2. (As a group, use a piece of newsprint or poster board to chart out Peter's transformation.) Ask: **When did Peter become inwardly motivated?**
3. Discuss: **Are you inwardly motivated? When did that happen? How did it happen?**
4. Summarize the different phases of leadership described in this and the previous session. Discuss each of those principles by asking, **How can you put this principle into action?**
5. Have each group member share the name of the student he would like to get closer to. (Work out any overlaps as a group and pray that each leader will be able to sustain the relationship until he has gone through all four leadership principles with the student he has selected.)

Session 19

1. Divide into two groups with older leaders in one group and younger leaders in the other. Have each group come up with a skit about what life was like when they were in high school. Allow five minutes for preparation. Encourage creativity with existing props. Each skit should be at least two minutes long.
2. Have the same two groups come up with a written definition of a Touch Ministry. Reassemble and discuss both definitions.
3. Let volunteers respond to (and discuss) each question on the Action Point for this session.
4. Assign volunteers to bring to the next session a yearbook, calendar, and newspaper from the school(s) your students attend.
5. Close the meeting by praying for each school and for the specific students you know who attend there.

Session 20

1. Have each person list five adjectives he would use to describe today's student culture.
2. Discuss: **What scares you most about getting to know students?**
3. Have each person select the one characteristic or element of a Touch Ministry that he needs to develop and explain why he needs that particular one.
4. Using the materials your volunteers collected (school annual, calendar, and newspaper), compile as much information as possible about the schools in your area.
5. Ask: **What steps do you need to take to start being involved in a Touch Ministry?** Have each person share the one step he will take this week.
6. Have each person name one student he can get to know through a Touch Ministry and one activity he can take part in to involve him with that student.

Session 21

1. Read 2 Timothy 2:2 aloud as a group. Have each person point out one element of discipleship described in the session material and write that element on a chalkboard or poster board. (Make sure the elements are listed in a single column.) Then discuss the central focus of each element. Write the central focus beside each principle.
2. Discuss the following questions:
   ■ (From the section on "Relationships")—**What do you find easiest about forming close relationships? What is hardest? How will your attitude toward close relationships help or hinder your efforts to disciple students?**
   ■ (From the section on "Reflection")—**How can you develop a trusting relationship with students? What obstacles might you face?**
   ■ (From the section on "Reality")—**Can you recall a time when you "blew it" in front of students? What happened? How did you feel? How can your vulnerability be turned into a positive experience?**
   ■ (From the section on "Recruiting")—**Why is it important to recruit F-A-T students? Who are the F-A-T students in your youth group?**
   ■ (From the section on "Reproduction")—**As you consider the four levels of discipleship referred to in 2 Timothy 2:2, how do you imagine God might use you to disciple students in a way that will have an impact on the generations to follow?**
3. Ask each person: **What do you think are the advantages and disadvantages of becoming a disciple-maker?**

Session 22

1. Read together Matthew 28:18-20. Write on poster board or a chalkboard the "four steps to making disciples."
2. Discuss the "Evangelize" step by listing the characteristics of Jesus' life from Matthew 9:35-38. How can those characteristics relate to your group members as they work with students?
3. Discuss the "Establish" step by using the wheel diagram to discuss the essential elements in establishing new Christians in their faith. Ask: **Why is each of these elements important?** Then examine the practical steps found in 1 Thessalonians 1:4-10 and discuss how Paul established those believers in their faith. How can you use those same steps in establishing students in Christ?
4. Discuss the "Equip" step by examining the prerequisites in 1 Thessalonians 2:4-12. Explain why you think each one is important in equipping students.
5. Discuss the "Extend" step by asking: **What effect do you think carrying out this stair-step process of discipling will have on your youth group?**

Session 23

1. Discuss: **In today's student culture, what are things students most like to do? How can we take the positive aspects of those activities and build them into a Christ-centered meeting designed to communicate the Gospel to students?**
2. Discuss: **How does the concept of The Big Event ministry compare to what we're doing now with students?**
3. Ask: **What changes could we make in our current structure to present Jesus Christ in a more appealing way (such as The Big Event)? What steps do we as youth leaders need to take to see those changes happen?**
4. Review the building blocks necessary to begin The Big Event ministry. For each one, evaluate how successfully your church is meeting that requirement.

Session 24

1. Read Ephesians 4:11-16 aloud to the group. Discuss: **Are you prepared to do what Paul describes in these verses? If not, what do you need to do to prepare yourself?**
2. Let each person discuss his "Personal Plan of Action" for putting the Reach Out Strategy into practice.
3. Discuss as a group the evaluation of the various areas of the Reach Out Strategy in terms of "where we are now" and "where we need to be."
4. Evaluate the students in your youth ministry using your

group members' answers to *Action Point* questions #4 and #5.

Session 25

1. Have each group member read his response to Question #2 of the *Action Point*. Take time to clarify any questions your group might have.
2. Ask: **What are some aspects of God's purpose for you that would be common to all Christians?** Write down all responses and then as a group come up with a definition for "God's purpose for your life."
3. Have volunteers share their dreams of God glorifying Himself through their lives.
4. Have each member share one illustration to confirm that God has already begun to accomplish His purpose in him.

Session 26

1. Read Jeremiah 29:11-13. Have each person express his thoughts on how "loving God with all your heart, with all your soul, and with all your strength" fits into his dream of glorifying God.
2. Have volunteers share an experience where they have been faced with the choice of following their own goals or God's goals for their life. Ask them to be personal and specific.
3. Ask: **Why do you think Jesus said that the greatest commandment is to love God with all your heart, soul, mind, and strength?**
4. Ask every group member to share his spiritual goals from the Personal Objectives Section. Do the same thing with each other area (social, mental, and physical).
5. Have everyone pair up and express to one another the first step toward accomplishing one of their personal goals this week. Have them pray for one another about overall goals, and then specifically that they would be able to accomplish the first step.

Session 27

1. Have each group member share what he did this week toward accomplishing one of his personal objectives (spiritual, social, mental, or physical).
2. Ask: **Why do you think Jesus said that loving your neighbor as yourself was the second greatest commandment?**
3. Ask if anyone has questions about developing his goals for loving his family and friends.
4. Let each person share his family objectives. Then repeat the process with the friendship objectives.
5. Pair up the same partners who met during the last session. Have each person express the first step he will take toward

accomplishing one of his goals for family or friends. Have partners pray for one another about overall goals and then specifically for their first steps to be taken this week.

Session 28

1. Have each group member share what he did this last week toward accomplishing one family or friendship objective.
2. Discuss any questions members may have about developing goals for job and church.
3. Have each person share his job objectives. Then repeat the process with church ministry objectives.
4. Pair up the same partners who met during the past couple of sessions. Partners should share the first step they will take toward accomplishing one of their goals for job or church, and then pray for one another.
5. Tell group members to expect to take more time than normal to complete the next session. They should get started early in the week, because they will be beginning the process of seeing their dreams and objectives accomplished.

Session 29

1. Have each group member share what he did this last week toward accomplishing one job or church ministry objective.
2. Discuss: **What struggles do you face in trying to live a "balanced life"?** Summarize: **It will always be a struggle to maintain a balanced lifestyle. Yet without determining our lifetime goals, our one-year goals, and then working those goals into our daily schedules, a balanced lifestyle would always be an illusive dream.**
3. Use one of your lifetime goals as an example to show the group how to work out their one-year goals. Using a chalkboard or poster board, outline the steps you went through to convert that lifetime goal into a yearly goal.
4. Show the group how you determined whether some of your yearly goals should be "A," "B," or "C" priorities.
5. Have each group member spend a few minutes reviewing the one-year goals he wrote from his lifetime goals to see if he would like to revise one or more of them.
6. Once again, pair up the people who have been partners for the past several sessions. One person should select a one-year objective to share. The other person should critique that goal. (Is it what God wants? Is it measurable? Can it be completed in a year?) Then have the first partner critique one of the second person's goals. Finally, have partners pray for wisdom as they begin to work toward accomplishing their one-year objectives.

Session 30 (Group Project)

Prior to the group meeting:

1. Write out the long-term goals of your youth ministry. If you are not the youth minister, meet with him to work out these goals.
2. Using your list of long-term goals, determine the one-year goals for your youth ministry. Prioritize these one-year goals using the "A," "B," and "C" ratings.
3. Use a calendar for the next year and chart out how you intend to accomplish your one-year goals.
4. Draw up a tentative weekly schedule for your youth ministry based on your calendar.
5. Prepare copies (2 per person) of the Daily Time Log that group members can use to project their Ideal Weekly Schedules and proposed schedules for the coming week.

During the group meeting:

6. Be prepared to evaluate group members' proposed schedules for the coming week. (See Session 30.)
7. Establish which group member(s) will be responsible to carry out each activity listed on the youth ministry schedule. Also establish the activities each group member will be committed to attending.

Session 31

1. Have everyone share the best thing he got out of last week's project.
2. Work your way through the spiritual gifts list from this week's *Action Point.* Read each passage of Scripture and discuss the various gifts under each category.
3. Have a time of open discussion about spiritual gifts. Encourage questions and participation from group members.
4. Have each person answer these questions: **What do you think your motivation (grace) gift is? How do you think your gift can operate in youth ministry? How can you maximize the use of your gift?**
5. Have each group member pray for the person on his left. Pray that each person's spiritual gift will be used and manifested to God's glory in youth ministry.

Session 32

1. Have everyone share his greatest barrier in witnessing and explain why.
2. Have everyone report on his conversation with a non-Christian.
3. Have two volunteers role play a conversation between a Christian and a non-Christian ending at the point where the non-Christian receives Christ.
4. Ask group members to pair off and go through the same

conversation step by step (with you as the leader guiding them through each step).

5. Reassign partners, this time pairing one person who is experienced at witnessing with another person who isn't. Have partners compare schedules for the following week and find a time to go out and talk to some of the people on their Prayer Triangles.

6. Have partners pray for the people in the Prayer Triangles. They should concentrate on praying for the people they want to see this week.

Session 33

1. Discuss: **What should be our personal roles in following up new Christians?**

2. Pair up and go through each of the four follow-up sessions. Have one person lead the first and third sessions and the other lead the second and fourth. The nonleader needs to challenge the leader with any questions a new Christian would ask.

3. Discuss questions that were raised during the previous exercise. If questions are raised that don't relate to following up on a new Christian, defer them to a later time.

4. Discuss whether or not your ministry or church has an effective plan for following up new Christians. If the answer is no, consider using the tools offered by the Moving Toward Maturity series (Barry St. Clair, Victor) as your plan. (You may want to have available sample materials for the group to consider.)

Session 34

1. Have the group think of one student (that most of them know) who went to your church during high school and since graduated. Discuss: **Would you consider that student a "discipled" student? On what basis would you make that judgment?**

2. From the previous study of 1 Thessalonians 1, have the group come up with a list of qualities for a discipled student.

3. From the previous study of 1 Thessalonians 2, have the group come up with a list of desired qualities for a person who disciples students.

4. From the Profile of a Disciple, come up with a list of the top four or five qualities your youth ministry wants to develop in your students' lives. Why did you choose those particular qualities? (Discuss as a group.)

5. Discuss: **What do we need to do as a leadership group and individually to develop those qualities in the students who are a part of our ministry right now?**

Session 35

(Note: You may wish to invite a Christian counselor whom you respect to take part in this meeting.)

1. Set up a counseling situation that your group members can relate to. (Example: A girl is pregnant and comes to you for counseling on whether or not to have an abortion.)

2. Let the group discuss how to counsel the girl. Ask the following questions as the discussion continues:
   What is the "fruit" of this issue?
   How do we get to the "root" of the problem?
   How do we identify the "root" of her problem?
   (Rejection, fear, etc.)
   What are some solutions to the problem?
   How would you help her see the solution?
   How will you know when the problem is solved?
   Whom will she be accountable to in order to get this problem worked out?
   What can you do to help her be accountable?

3. Pray that God will give each of you the wisdom and insight to move beyond the "fruit" and down to the "root" to help students solve their problems.

[NOTE: In preparing for next week, you need to go ahead and look at the discussion questions now. If you decide to have everyone bring a token gift for each person, you need to announce it during this week's meeting.]

Session 36

1. Role play a skit where a leader is trying to teach the following characters in a small group:
   ■ Nelly Nurse (Replies "It's OK" every time someone tries to share a problem)
   ■ Andy Answers (Has an answer for every question)
   ■ Silent Sam (Doesn't ever say anything)
   ■ Danny Dominant (Talks all the time)
   After a few minutes of role play, stop and discuss how to effectively handle each character. Discuss ways to take a situation like this and turn it into a positive group discussion.

2. Discuss: **What are the top five needs in a small group?**

3. Let each person share the two greatest benefits he has received from being in a small group.

4. Select one person in the group and let all the other members express the one thing about that person that means the most to them. Then go on to the next person and do the same thing until everyone has been covered. (Option: Have everyone bring small gifts for the other members of the group and exchange them at this final meeting.)

5. Close in prayer, asking God to help each person use what he has learned during this study to increase the effectiveness of his ministry.

☐ ADDITIONAL RESOURCES

The following resources are not required for each session's study, but they will provide much information and insight if you choose to examine them during your study of *Leadership!*

SESSION 1—(Group project)

SESSION 2

Many Aspire, Few Attain (Walter A. Henrichsen, Navpress)

Tyranny of the Urgent (Charles Hummel, InterVarsity Press)

SESSION 3

Dedication and Leadership (Douglas Hyde, University of Notre Dame Press)

SESSION 4

"Have You Heard of the Four Spiritual Laws?" (Tract by Campus Crusade for Christ)

New Life (Andrew Murray, Bethany House)

My Heart, Christ's Home (Dr. Robert B. Munger, InterVarsity Press)

"Biblical Salvation" (A cassette tape by Jack Taylor, available from Reach Out Ministries)

SESSION 5

How to Experience God's Love and Forgiveness (Bill Bright, Here's Life Publishers)

Love Is Now (Peter E. Gillquist, Zondervan)

Love, Acceptance, and Forgiveness (Jerry Cook and Stanley C. Baldwin, Regal Books)

Three Kinds of Love (M. Toyotome, InterVarsity Press)

SESSION 6

Pursuit of Holiness (Jerry Bridges, Navpress)

"Spiritual Leadership" (A cassette tape by Barry St. Clair, available from Reach Out Ministries)

Continuous Revival (Norman Grubb, Christian Literature Crusade)

SESSION 7

On Tiptoe With Love (John T. Seamands, Baker Book House)

Spirit Filled Life (Pamphlet by Campus Crusade for Christ)

Be Filled Now (Roy Hession, Christian Literature Crusade)

SESSION 8

The Key to Triumphant Living (Jack Taylor, Broadman Press)

The Normal Christian Life (Watchman Nee, Tyndale)

SESSION 9

Time Alone with God (A booklet by Barry St. Clair, available from Reach Out Ministries)

Manna in the Morning (A booklet by Stephen Olford, available from Encounter Ministries, Wheaton, IL 60189)

"Knowing God" (A cassette tape series by Peter Lord, available from Reach Out Ministries)

SESSION 10

The Joy of Discovery in Bible Study (Oletta Wald, Augsburg)

"How to Make Bible Study Exciting" (A cassette tape by Barry St. Clair, available from Reach Out Ministries)

SESSION 11

"Scripture Memory" (A cassette tape by Barry St. Clair, available from Reach Out Ministries)

Meditation (Jim Downing, Navpress)

SESSION 12

"Powerful Prayer" (A cassette tape by Barry St. Clair, available from Reach Out Ministries)

Acts in Prayer (E. W. Price, Jr., Broadman Press)

With Christ in the School of Prayer (Andrew Murray, Revell)

With Concerts of Prayer (David Bryant, Regal)

SESSION 13—(Group project)

SESSION 14

Reach Out Strategy Workbook (Barry St. Clair, available from Reach Out Ministries)

The Master Plan of Evangelism (Robert Coleman, Revell)

SESSION 15

Jesus Is Lord (A booklet by Barry St. Clair, available from Reach Out Ministries)

Continuous Revival (Norman Grubb, Christian Literature Crusade)

Calvary Road (Roy Hession, Christian Literature Crusade)

SESSION 16

We Would See Jesus (Roy Hession, Christian Literature Crusade)

Victory Through Surrender (E. Stanley Jones, Abingdon)

SESSION 17

Spiritual Leadership (Oswald Sanders, Moody Press)

Be the Leader You Were Meant to Be (Leroy Eims, Victor Books)

SESSION 18

Dedication and Leadership (Douglas Hyde, University of

Notre Dame Press)

"Leadership and Motivation" (Cassette tapes by Howard Hendricks, available from Campus Crusade for Christ)

The Making of a Man of God (Alan Redpath, Revell)

SESSION 19

Giving Away Your Faith (Barry St. Clair, Victor Books)

Winning Ways (Leroy Eims, Victor Books)

Life-Style Evangelism (Joseph C. Aldrich, Multnomah Press)

SESSION 20

Out of the Salt Shaker (Rebecca Pippert, InterVarsity Press)

How to Give Away Your Faith (Paul E. Little, InterVarsity Press)

SESSION 21

Discipleship: A Ministry Imperative (Barry St. Clair, available from Reach Out Ministries)

"Moving Toward Maturity" series (Barry St. Clair, Victor Books, [Note: This is a five-book discipleship series which includes *Following Jesus, Spending Time Alone with God, Making Jesus Lord, Giving Away Your Faith,* and *Influencing Your World.*]

Discipleship: The Best Writings from the Most Experienced Disciple Makers (edited by William Shell, Zondervan)

SESSION 22

Born to Reproduce (Dawson Trotman, Navpress)

The Lost Art of Disciple Making (Leroy Eims, Zondervan)

Disciples Are Made—Not Born (Walter Henrichsen, Victor)

SESSION 23

Joy Explosion (Barry St. Clair, Victor Books)

Ideas (Youth Specialties)

SESSION 24

Reach Out Strategy Workbook (Barry St. Clair, available from Reach Out Ministries)

SESSION 25

In His Image (Dr. Paul Brand and Philip Yancey, Zondervan)

SESSIONS 26-28

Strategy for Living (Edward R. Rayton and Ted Engstrom, Regal)

The One Minute Manager (Kenneth Blanchard and Spencer Johnson, Morrow)

The Christian Executive (Edward R. Dayton and Ted Engstrom, Word)

SESSION 29

"Time Management" (Cassette tapes by Merill Douglas and Larry Baker, 7300 N. Lehigh Ave., Chicago, IL 60648.)

SESSION 30—(Group project)

SESSION 31

Discover Your Spiritual Gift and Use It (Rick Yohn, Tyndale)

Unwrap Your Spiritual Gifts (Kenneth O. Gangel, Victor Books)

SESSION 32

Lifestyle Evangelism (Joseph C. Aldrich, Multnomah Press)

Winning Ways (Leroy Eims, Victor Books)

Out of the Salt Shaker (Rebecca Pippert, InterVarsity Press)

SESSION 33

The Dynamics of Personal Follow Up (Gary Kuhne, Zondervan)

The Big Man on Campus (Barry St. Clair, Victor Books)

The Fight (John White, InterVarsity Press)

SESSION 34

The Master Plan of Evangelism (Robert Coleman, Revell)

Disciples Are Made—Not Born (Walter Henrichsen, Victor Books)

Discipleship: A Ministry Imperative (Barry St. Clair, available from Reach Out Ministries)

SESSION 35

Effective Biblical Counseling (Lawrence J. Crabb, Jr., Zondervan)

Basic Principles of Biblical Counseling (Lawrence J. Crabb, Jr., Zondervan)

The Ins and Outs of Rejection (Charles R. Solomon, Heritage House)

SESSION 36

69 Ways to Start a Study Group (Larry Richards, Zondervan)

Growing Together in Small Groups (Em Griffin, InterVarsity Press)

All materials available from Reach Out Ministries can be obtained by writing:

Reach Out Ministries
3961 Holcomb Bridge Road, Suite 201
Norcross, GA 30092

CHECK-OFF SHEET FOR *LEADERSHIP!* ASSIGNMENTS

(Note: Assignments are to be completed during the week *following* the session indicated.)

SESSION	COMPLETE NEXT SESSION	SCRIPTURE MEMORY	DAILY TIME ALONE WITH GOD (Readings below are from the Book of Mark.)						
			DAY 1	DAY 2	DAY 3	DAY 4	DAY 5	DAY 6	DAY 7
1									
2									
3									
4									
5									
6									
7									
8									
9			Begin to spend 20 minutes with God each day this week.						
10			1:1-3	1:4-8	1:9-13	1:14-15	1:16-20	1:21-26	1:27-28
11		2 Timothy 3:16	1:29-31	1:32-34	1:35-39	1:40-45	2:1-5	2:6-7	2:8-12
12		John 15:7	2:13-14	2:15-17	2:18-20	2:21-22	2:23-26	2:27-28	3:1-2
13		Review previous verses	3:3-6	3:7-8	3:9-10	3:1-12	3:13-19	3:20-21	3:22-23
14		Mark 1:17	3:24-26	3:27-30	3:31-35	4:1-4	4:5-6	4:7-9	4:10-12
15		Philippians 2:9-11	4:13-14	4:15-20	4:21-23	4:24-25	4:26-29	4:30-32	4:33-34
16		Matthew 16:24	4:35-41	5:1-5	5:6-8	5:9-10	5:11-13	5:14-17	5:18-20
17		2 Corinthians 12:9	5:21-24	5:25-29	5:30-34	5:35-36	5:37-40	5:41-43	6:1-3
18		1 Thessalonians 2:19	6:4-6	6:7-11	6:12-13	6:14-20	6:21-25	6:26-29	6:30-34
19		Matthew 9:37-38	6:35-37	6:38-44	6:45-52	6:53-56	7:1-5	7:6-8	7:9-13
20		1 Thessalonians 2:8	7:14-16	7:17-19	7:20-23	7:24-25	7:26-30	7:31-35	7:36-37
21		2 Timothy 2:2	8:1-3	8:4-10	8:11-13	8:14-16	8:17-21	8:22-26	8:27-30
22		Matthew 28:18-20	8:31-33	8:34-35	8:36—9:1	9:2-4	9:5-8	9:9-13	9:14-15
23		John 7:37-38	9:16-19	9:20-24	9:25-27	9:28-32	9:33-37	9:38-41	9:42-48
24		Ephesians 4:11-13	9:49-50	10:1-9	10:11-12	10:13-16	10:17-20	10:21-23	10:24-27
25		1 Corinthians 10:31	10:28-31	10:32-34	10:35-40	10:41-45	10:46-52	11:1-3	11:4-6
26		Matthew 22:36-38	11:7-11	11:12-14	11:15-17	11:18-19	11:20-23	11:24-26	11:27-33
27		John 15:13	12:1-8	12:9-12	12:13-17	12:18-23	12:24-27	12:28-31	12:32-34
28		Acts 1:8	12:35-37	12:38-40	12:41-44	13:1-4	13:5-8	13:9-11	13:12-13
29		Ephesians 5:15-16	13:14-20	13:21-23	13:24-25	13:26-27	13:28-31	13:32-34	13:35-37
30		Review previous verses	14:1-2	14:3-5	14:6-9	14:10-11	14:12-16	14:17-21	14:22-26
31		1 Corinthians 12:11	14:27-31	14:32-36	14:37-38	14:39-40	14:41-42	14:43-47	14:48-52
32		Luke 19:10	14:53-56	14:57-59	14:60-65	14:66-72	15:1-5	15:6-11	15:12-15
33		1 Peter 2:2	15:16-20	15:21-24	15:25-32	15:33-36	15:37-41	15:42-45	15:46-47
34		Colossians 1:28-29	16:1-3	16:4-8	16:9-11	16:12-13	16:14-15	16:16-18	16:19-20
35		Ephesians 4:22-24	Continue daily Bible reading on your own.						
36		Hebrews 10:24-25							

Check off each assignment as you complete it. Soon you should begin to feel a sense of accomplishment with every check mark.

☐ TIME ALONE WITH GOD NOTEBOOK INSERTS

These sheets provide suggestions for beginning a time alone with God and daily outlines to keep it going strong.

Photocopy the pages and insert them in a 5½″ x 8½″ notebook. For a 10-week supply, make:
- 1 copy of pages 135-139
- 5 copies of page 140
- 10 copies of page 141

Contents of these inserts have been excerpted from *Spending Time Alone with God* (Book 2 of the Moving Toward Maturity series).

HOW TO STUDY A PASSAGE OF SCRIPTURE

OBSERVATION (Use with *Title* and *Key Verse* sections of your Bible Response Sheet.)

Pray first for the Holy Spirit's guidance, and then read the passage carefully. Read with an open mind, ready to receive and obey what God has to teach you.

INTERPRETATION (Use with the *Summary* section of your Bible Response Sheet.)

Step One – Read the verses preceding and following the passage in order to understand the proper setting and context.

Step Two – Ask yourself these questions about the passage: *Who? What? When? Where? Why?* and *How?* Write down your insights and any unanswered questions you may have.

Step Three – Look up unfamiliar terms in a standard dictionary or a Bible dictionary.

APPLICATION (Use with the *Personal Application* section of your Bible Response Sheet.)

Step One – Look for:

Promises to claim	*Commands* to obey
Attitudes to change	*Actions* to take
Challenges to accept	*Examples* to follow
Sins to confess	*Skills* to learn

Step Two – Describe how the passage applies to your life by asking yourself these questions: "How can I make this passage personal?" "How can I make it practical?" "How can I make it measurable?" Be specific.

MEMORIZATION
Find a verse or passage of Scripture that speaks to you personally, and memorize it.

HOW TO HAVE A TIME ALONE WITH GOD

By the time you finish this book, your daily time alone with God will include Bible study, praise, thanksgiving, confession, petition, and intercession. Here is a guideline that will allow you to include all aspects of Bible reading and prayer within a 15-minute period of time.

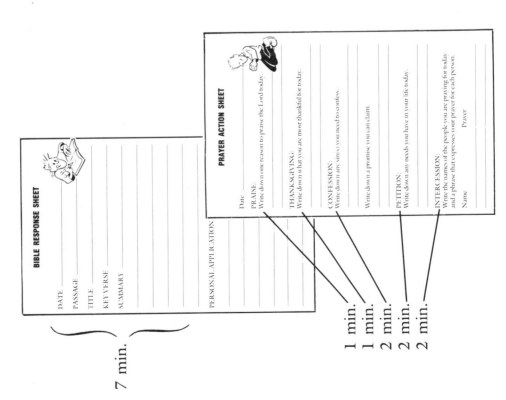

BIBLE RESPONSE SHEET

DATE
PASSAGE
TITLE
KEY VERSE
SUMMARY

7 min.

PERSONAL APPLICATION

PRAYER ACTION SHEET

Date
PRAISE:
Write down one reason to praise the Lord today.

THANKSGIVING:
Write down what you are most thankful for today.

CONFESSION:
Write down any sin(s) you need to confess.

Write down a promise you can claim.

PETITION:
Write down any needs you have in your life today.

INTERCESSION:
Write the names of the people you are praying for today and a phrase that expresses your prayer for each person.

Name   Prayer

1 min.
1 min.
2 min.
2 min.
2 min.

THIRTY DAYS OF PRAISE

Day 1:	Psalm 8	Day 16:	Psalm 104:1-23
Day 2:	Psalm 23	Day 17:	Psalm 104:24-35
Day 3:	Psalm 34:1-3; 50:1-6	Day 18:	Psalm 111
Day 4:	Psalm 63:1-4; 66:1-7	Day 19:	Psalm 112
Day 5:	Psalm 67	Day 20:	Psalm 113
Day 6:	Psalm 84	Day 21:	Psalm 134
Day 7:	Psalm 86	Day 22:	Psalm 135:1-7
Day 8:	Psalm 90	Day 23:	Psalm 138
Day 9:	Psalm 91	Day 24:	Psalm 139
Day 10:	Psalm 92	Day 25:	Psalm 145
Day 11:	Psalm 93	Day 26:	Psalm 146
Day 12:	Psalm 95:1-7	Day 27:	Psalm 147
Day 13:	Psalm 96	Day 28:	Psalm 148
Day 14:	Psalm 100	Day 29:	Psalm 149
Day 15:	Psalm 103	Day 30:	Psalm 150

SEVEN DAYS OF THANKSGIVING

Focus your thanks to the Lord in two areas each day: (1) Bible passages that describe His promises and gifts to you, and (2) your personal thanks for God's working in your daily life.

Day 1
Pray through 2 Peter 1:4 to express your thanks to God.

Lord, thank You for Your great and precious promises that You have given to me that I might be part of Your divine nature.

I also thank You for:
Your amazing love,
letting me be in Your family,
making me really live, and
life at its most fantastic in Jesus.

HOW TO MEMORIZE SCRIPTURE

READ THE PASSAGE SEVERAL TIMES. First read it silently, and then aloud.

UNDERSTAND THE PASSAGE.

Read it in the context of the passages around it.
Read the comments about the verse in a Bible commentary (for example, *Wycliffe Bible Commentary*).
Write in a few words what the passage is about.

VISUALIZE THE PASSAGE. Use your imagination to picture the passage. For example, Matthew 5:1-12 is part of the "Sermon on the Mount." Picture yourself there on the mountain with Jesus. Then place each of these "Beatitudes" on the side of the mountain. Later, that picture will come to mind and help you recall these verses.

BREAK DOWN THE PASSAGE INTO NATURAL PHRASES. Learn the first phrase of the passage; then add the second. Continue adding phrases until you have memorized the entire passage.

LEARN THE REFERENCE AS PART OF THE PASSAGE. Say the reference, then the verse, and then repeat the reference again at the end. This step helps you fix the location of the verse in your mind, allowing you to turn to it immediately when you need it.

LEARN IT WORD PERFECT. As you are saying the passage over and over to yourself, continue to correct yourself until you've learned it exactly as it is written. You are already taking the time to learn it, so why not do it right! Learning it this way now will give you confidence to quote and use the passage later.

MEDITATE ON THE PASSAGE. As you think and pray about the passage, ask God to speak to you. When the passage becomes meaningful to you, then it will be much easier for you to remember.

REVIEW THE PASSAGE. Each day, review the Scripture passages you have already learned. If you review a passage every day for 30 days, it will be very difficult to forget.

Day 2
Pray through 1 John 1:7 and Colossians 1:14 to express your thanks to God.

Father, I thank You for the blood of Your Son Jesus Christ that cleanses me from all sin and frees me from Satan's power.

I also thank You for:
Your patience,
Your comfort,
Your closeness to me,
Your disciplining of me, and
Your love inside me.

Day 3
Pray through 1 Peter 2:24 to express your thanks to God.

Lord Jesus, I thank You that You bore my sins in Your body on the cross, so that I can die to sin and live righteously, and that by Your wounds I am healed.

I also thank You for:
the body of Christ (other Christians),
the privilege of prayer,
my home, and
my parents.

Day 4
Pray through Ephesians 2:8-10 to express your thanks to God.

Lord, I thank You that I am saved by grace through faith, and that it is Your free gift — I don't have to work for it. But thank You that, as Your new creation, I can live for You and help others.

I also thank You for:
my body,
my health,
my strength,
happy times,
sad times, and
in-between times.

Day 5
Pray through Psalm 91:11-14 to express your thanks to God.

Lord, I thank You that You give Your angels charge over me to guard me in all my ways. They will steady me with their hands and protect me. You will deliver me because I love You.

I also thank You for:
opportunities for spiritual growth,
comfort when I'm depressed,
joy when I'm sad, and
courage when I'm scared.

Day 6
Pray through Ephesians 1:3-6 to express your thanks to God.

Lord, thank You for choosing me to be adopted into Your family. Thank You for blessing me with all the good things You have stored up for those who belong to Christ.

I also thank You for:
food,
clothes,
a place to live,
freedom to say what I feel, and
freedom not to say what I feel.

Day 7
Pray through 2 Corinthians 8:9 and 9:8 to express your thanks to God.

Thank You, Lord, for paying a debt for me (my debt of sin) that I could never have repaid. Thank You not only for saving me from sin but for giving me the grace I need today to live for You.

I also thank You for:
saving me from selfishness,
saving me from pride, and
saving me from eternal separation from You.

THIRTY DAYS OF CONFESSION

Sins to Confess:

Day 1: 2 Timothy 2:22. Do you have impure thoughts?
Day 2: Philippians 2:14-15. Do you complain or gripe?
Day 3: Ephesians 6:1-3. Do you honor your parents?
Day 4: Ephesians 4:31. Are you bitter toward anyone?
Day 5: 1 Corinthians 6:19-20. Are you careless with your body?
Day 6: Matthew 6:33. Do you seek what God wants first?
Day 7: Matthew 6:14. Do you have a bad attitude toward someone?
Day 8: 2 Timothy 2:22. Do you have impure motives?
Day 9: Colossians 3:9. Do you lie?
Day 10: Ephesians 6:1-3. Do you respect your parents?
Day 11: Ephesians 4:31. Is there anger in your life?
Day 12: 1 Corinthians 6:19-20. Do you have bad habits?
Day 13: Matthew 6:33. Is God the most important person in your life?
Day 14: Matthew 6:14. Are you holding a grudge?
Day 15: 2 Timothy 2:22. Are your thoughts pure toward the opposite sex?
Day 16: Philippians 2:14-15. Do you have a critical attitude?
Day 17: Colossians 3:9. Do you steal?
Day 18: Ephesians 4:31. Do you talk about others behind their backs?
Day 19: 1 Corinthians 6:19-20. Are you lazy?
Day 20: Matthew 6:33. Have you given God everything in your life?
Day 21: Matthew 6:14. Do you have a wrong relationship with someone?
Day 22: Colossians 3:9. Do you cheat in school?
Day 23: Ephesians 6:1-3. Do you have problems with authority?
Day 24: Ephesians 4:31. Are you jealous of anyone?
Day 25: 1 Corinthians 6:19-20. Do you eat too much?
Day 26: Matthew 6:33. Are you trusting God with your life?
Day 27: Matthew 6:14. Is there anyone you resent?
Day 28: Philippians 2:14-15. Does your attitude honor God?
Day 29: Ephesians 6:1-3. Are you rebellious?
Day 30: Ephesians 4:31. Do you argue with other people?

Promises to Claim:

Day 1: Philippians 4:8
Day 2: Psalm 119:9
Day 3: Colossians 3:9-10
Day 4: Galatians 2:20
Day 5: Colossians 3:20
Day 6: 1 John 4:7
Day 7: Hebrews 12:15
Day 8: Ephesians 4:29
Day 9: 1 Corinthians 6:13
Day 10: Colossians 1:27
Day 11: Luke 9:23
Day 12: 2 Corinthians 9:8
Day 13: 1 John 4:4
Day 14: Philippians 1:9
Day 15: 2 Thessalonians 1:12
Day 16: 1 Corinthians 10:13
Day 17: 1 Thessalonians 4:3
Day 18: Ephesians 2:10
Day 19: Colossians 1:13
Day 20: Ephesians 6:2
Day 21: Galatians 5:18
Day 22: Ephesians 4:26
Day 23: 1 Corinthians 3:16
Day 24: Romans 12:1
Day 25: 2 Corinthians 5:17
Day 26: Philippians 2:5-7
Day 27: Matthew 6:12
Day 28: Ephesians 1:3-7
Day 29: Colossians 2:2-3
Day 30: Philippians 3:1

These sins to confess and promises to claim will help you through your first 30 days of confession. During the first month, you will discover several areas God wants to change in your life. From then on, follow the passage that corresponds to that day of the month. Apply it to a sin you need to confess or promise you need to claim.

SEVEN DAYS OF PETITION

Focus your petitions in two areas each day: (1) Bible passages that describe what God wants for you, and (2) your personal requests for God to supply your needs.

DAY 1
(Read Galatians 2:20.)
"Jesus, help me to live as someone who is dead to my own selfish desires. Take charge of my body, my mind, and my emotions. Live Your life in me today."

Other needs:

DAY 2
(Read Galatians 5:22-23.)
"Jesus, please help my life to express these qualities to other people."

PRAYERS YOU CAN PRAY FOR OTHERS

Look at these prayers of the Apostle Paul. They will help you know how to pray for other people. In fact, you can pray these specific prayers for them.

"And this is my prayer: that your love may abound more and more in knowledge and depth of insight, so that you may be able to discern what is best and may be pure and blameless until the day of Christ, filled with the fruit of righteousness that comes through Jesus Christ — to the glory and praise of God" (Philippians 1:9-11).

"I pray that out of His glorious riches He may strengthen you with power through His Spirit in your inner being, so that Christ may dwell in your hearts through faith. And I pray that you, being rooted and established in love, may have power, together with all the saints, to grasp how wide and long and high and deep is the love of Christ, and to know this love that surpasses knowledge — that you may be filled to the measure of all the fullness of God" (Ephesians 3:16-19).

"We always thank God for all of you, mentioning you in our prayers. We continually remember before our God and Father your work produced by faith, your labor prompted by love, and your endurance inspired by hope in our Lord Jesus Christ" (1 Thessalonians 1:2-3).

Other needs: _____

DAY 3
(Read Ephesians 5:18.)
"Jesus, I claim the filling of Your Spirit. Fill me now. I pray for all that comes from Your Spirit: courage, power, wisdom, sexual purity, boldness, compassion, enthusiasm, honesty, and openness."

Other needs: _____

DAY 4
(Read 1 Corinthians 12:4-6.)
"Lord, help me to know my spiritual gift(s) and use it for Your glory."

Other needs: _____

DAY 5
(Read Ephesians 6:10-17.)
"Jesus, it's tough to be a Christian in this world. The pressure gets heavy at times. I ask for Your strength and protection. I put on Your armor: the belt of truth, the breastplate of righteousness, the shoes of the Gospel of peace, the shield of faith, the helmet of salvation, and the sword of the Spirit — the Word of God."

Other needs: _____

DAY 6
(Read Isaiah 41:10.)
"Lord, sometimes I am afraid. But I know I don't have to get scared because You are my help and my strength. Help me today to overcome fear by trusting in You."

Other needs: _____

DAY 7
(Read Acts 1:8.)
"Jesus, I want to be a witness for You to my friends. Give me the power and courage to be Your witness today."

Other needs: _____

RECORD OF INTERCESSION

As you begin to pray for other people, use a form like the one below to: (1) record the things you are praying for each person, and (2) help you keep up with God's answers to your prayers. Fill in the person's name at the top (Mom, Dad, sister, brother, friend, etc.). Don't try to pray for everyone every day—just a few people each day is enough.

Name _____

Date Prayed	Request	Answer	Date Answered

RECORD OF PETITION

As you begin to pray for yourself, use a form like the one below to: (1) record the things you are praying for, and (2) help you keep up with God's answers to those prayers.

NEEDS FOR MY LIFE

Date Prayed	Request	Answer	Date Answered

PRAYER ACTION SHEET

Date _____

PRAISE:
Write down one reason to praise the Lord today.

_____
_____

THANKSGIVING:
Write down what you are most thankful for today.

_____
_____

CONFESSION:
Write down any sin(s) you need to confess.

_____
_____

Write down a promise you can claim.

_____
_____

PETITION:
Write down any needs you have in your life today.

_____
_____

INTERCESSION:
Write the names of the people you are praying for today
and a phrase that expresses your prayer for each person.

Name   Prayer

_____

BIBLE RESPONSE SHEET

DATE _____

PASSAGE _____

TITLE _____

KEY VERSE _____

SUMMARY _____
_____
_____
_____
_____

PERSONAL APPLICATION _____
_____
_____
_____

Other resources by Barry St. Clair that will help you in your personal growth and ministry:

Moving Toward Maturity Series
- *Following Jesus* (Book 1) examines what it really means to follow Christ, and helps students grasp the basics of Christian living.
- *Spending Time Alone with God* (Book 2) provides a plan to motivate students in personal prayer and Bible study.
- *Making Jesus Lord* (Book 3) relates the Trinity to the gut-level issues that students face today, like dating, sex, parents, and peer pressure. Helps students discover how to make Jesus Lord.
- *Giving Away Your Faith* (Book 4) teaches students to live and speak as followers of Christ. Also helpful in preparation for missions work.
- *Influencing Your World* (Book 5) prepares students to become servants, disciple-makers, and spiritual leaders.

The Youth Ministry Puzzle Video. This video package takes a serious look at the essential ingredients for a youth ministry strategy in the local church. Youth workers and leaders can view and discuss together this presentation of effective youth ministry strategy taught by Barry St. Clair.

The Facts of Life. Talking to friends about Jesus Christ is one of the greatest challenges Christians face at school. This booklet, written specifically to reach young people, is a dynamic tool for outreach.

Getting Started. An excellent booklet to give to a new Christian. Its hard-hitting approach will help a new believer know what steps to take to follow Christ. And it provides positive answers to how to communicate their new found faith to their parents and friends.

Time Alone with God Notebook. This notebook is for use in your personal quiet time. Each notebook has a 10-week supply of application-oriented material.